Bickers and Son

Anderida - Or the Briton and the Saxon - A.D. CCCCXLI

Vol. II

ANDERIDA;

OR,

THE BRITON AND THE SAXON,

A.D. CCCCXLI.

IN THREE VOLUMES.

VOL. II.

LONDON:

BICKERS AND SON,

1, LEICESTER SQUARE.

1875.

ANDERIDA.

CHAPTER I.

ARE our pleasures greater in proportion to the pains we take to procure them? Is joy enhanced by the sorrow we have passed through in reaching it? Do we appreciate happiness according to the price paid for it? If not, what fools we are to scheme and toil in hope of carrying a heavier burden. Can a man rising from a luxurious banquet truly say that the costly viands have yielded him more enjoyment than is felt by him who satisfies healthy hunger with simple food? Is the brilliant festival, prolonged into the morning with music and dancing, with rich colours and sweet odours, with flowers and lights and gems—is the gaudy pomp more delicious than standing on the cliff of some high southern promontory when the south-wester blows freshly over a thousand leagues of salt water, and the sea-mews cry their orisons to the sun as he rests on the restless sea?

What price do the young pay for the healthy vigour which requires labour and hardship and danger to counterpoise its buoyancy? We eat simple food long without cloying; the simple pleasures of children are the most vivid and enduring; the complex machine soonest breaks down. All this is truth of truism, the commonest of commonplace. Did not the fathers show us this with laborious style and balanced phrase? Yet still, to be as foolish as one's neighbour is the standard of average aspiration, and supreme bliss consists in being able to surpass him in extravagance.

The Bishop of Anderida and Comail were discussing this question as it bore upon hunting. The former asserted that sport is not to be had without attendants for various functions—huntsmen and drivers, hounds of diverse qualities, horns and holas, and all appointed ceremony and apparatus of former times.

" When a boy stones a cat in an orchard," he said, " that is not sport."

" Not for the cat," answered Comail, "but probably the boy considers it very good sport; however that may be, the addition of ten others, with whistles and green ribbons and antic gestures, would not make it more so. But when a man, alone or with his hounds, pursues the winter wolf, and by address, patience, and courage, brings him to bay and kills him, that man, with or without paraphernalia, is a hunter."

" Or a vermin-killer," repeated the bishop ; "all depends on the mode and method of the business. Every art has its rules and its degrees ; the greater the proficiency the higher the degree, but no one who wilfully violates the rules deserves to be called an artist. The perfect hunter must thoroughly know the nature and habits of the beast he chases; the powers of the instruments, animate or inanimate, which he employs; the signs on the earth or the water; of wind and weather. When one device or engine fails he must be ready with another. He must know what horse and hound and weapon to use on each occasion, and be perfect in the use. He must be able to blow the right note and give the right hola. He must be provided with garments and appliances suitable and approved. The experience of Mathusala, the prowess of Samson, the wisdom of Salamo, the patience of Job."

"The patience of Job is to be desired," interrupted Comail, "and many of the other qualifications you have named are more or less essential, but others have as much to do with hunting as combing the hair has to do with eating. It is becoming to comb and wash and array one's self decently before meat, but all that is no part of the meal. Platters and tables, spoons and napkins, mirth and music, are pleasant, but they are not dinner, and we can dine very well without any or all of them."

"There can be no dinner," said the bishop, raising his voice as the matter became more interesting ; "there can be no such thing as dinner without the decencies and conventions of life. Man may satisfy his hunger, but how ? Like the beasts that perish--- 'comparatus est jumentis insipientibus, et similis est illis.' The satisfaction of the eye has much to do with the gratification of the palate. Would you drink wine out of a bucket ? Salamo mentions the colour, the sparkling, the movement of wine in the goblet, in his advice to those 'qui student calicibus epotandis.' So of eating he tells us, 'melius vocari ad olera cum charitate, quam ad vitulum saginatum cum odio'— where 'charitas' implies the grace and good cookery which distinguish the meal of civilized man, and 'odium,' the detestable rudeness of the ignorant. The instance is very striking, for there are few things more disgusting than fat veal badly cooked."

"The bishop is eloquent, he is speaking Latin," said Vortipore to Farinmail, who rode a few paces ahead of the other two. " I will wager my chain against your torque that the matter of his speech is eating, or drinking, or both."

" I shall not risk my torque on such a chance," answered Farinmail ; "but let us inquire if it be so."

They checked their horses, and as they rode side by side, Vortipore asked—

"A sermon, Bishop ? What is the subject of the discourse ? "

" I was instructing this young man how much the outward form of a thing constitutes the inward idea, makes it that which we know it to be; and that he who neglects externals will be 'left with nothing to care for. This topic we were examining by the light of Salamo's doctrine concerning dinner."

"Well!" said Vortipore, "as the sun must be two hours high, and hereabouts the place where we should break our fast, the teaching of Salamo can be combined with the lessons of experience.

" I see smoke rising from the trees in front of us," exclaimed Farinmail. " Doubtless the outward form of food is in preparation there for the sustenance of our inward idea of breakfast."

" Aye !" said Comail, " but much beside food is necessary for that purpose. If I understand the doctrine of Salamo, there must be suitable appliances, cups and vessels of the right form, garments of the proper colour, not to speak of roof overhead, rushes underfoot, and many other details."

" If you are particular about rushes," retorted the bishop, " you may gather abundance of them hard by, and may make provision for future needs."

" The whole question is too difficult for me," Comail murmured. "Am I feeding or am I fasting when I snatch a morsel as I go, satisfying my hunger without any form whatever ? "

" Have you any notion, Bishop," said the Count, " to what part of the forest Gorr is leading us ? "

" He has turned and twisted about on purpose to confuse us. He is a knave who loves mystery when he is not about his knavery, that people may be baffled who think he is always in mischief, and may suspect at the wrong time. Nevertheless we have come on the whole rather west of north, in the direction of the great iron-furnaces, towards Pen y Coit, where we hunted a white hart years ago—an unlucky hunt it was."

"Absurd !" exclaimed Vortipore. "We are miles from Pen y Coit."

" We are," the bishop replied ; "but it is just such a day as when we went there last. How many years ago was it ? "

" The devil knows, who guided us thither," said Vortipore savagely.

" In case he should guide us there again, I will fill my larder, for I have not forgotten how hungry I was before I found my way to the iron-works."

As he said this, the bishop stuffed with provisions a sort of valise which was secured to his saddle, replenished with wine a capa-

cious leathern bottle, and carefully closed
its mouth. Most of the others followed his
example. When they thought of the way
they had come, the turns and returns, by
forest and swamp, by streams that crept like
oil, by fords deep and muddy, or an occasional
bridge made of flattened tree trunks, they
felt that they might be long on the road if
they had to find their way without a guide;
and hungry also, with empty pouches.

Again they mounted, the mules were re-
loaded, and they advanced slowly and with
difficulty. The clearings in the forest were
few and poor, inhabited by a dingy, savage
population. The wind, which had been light
early in the morning, now blew steadily and
sighed a chill foreboding of rain.

" This is intolerable," cried the Count ; " it
must be near noon, and still we plod on, as if
we were driving bullocks to market."

" It will be a wet market for us," said
Comail, " if I am a judge of weather signs in
these parts."

" If you will be advised by me," said the

bishop, " ride quickly forward and see what Gorr is doing. We know that he is a rogue, and if I am not blind and deaf he is fooling us now. I have just returned from tracking the deer and the hounds. More than once I saw from the marks that the stag might have been forced into open ground, which is nearer than I supposed. The note of preparation should have been sounded and the gaze-hounds held in readiness ; instead of this, Gorr turned into the wood again, and now they are in the deep ground."

" Come then, in God's name !" cried the Count. " If he is doing as you say, his back shall be skinned with the scourge."

They spurred on under the bishop's leading to a hillock, from which they could see the movements both of men and hounds. After a brief inspection, Gorr and the chief huntsman were sent for, but in spite of suspicious circumstances, Gorr managed to parry the Count's questions, spicing his answers plentifully with terms of art. He fared less happily in the bishop's hands.

"Why did you let the deer get back," asked the latter, "when you had him at the edge of the wood out yonder?"

"Never was near the edge of the wood," replied Gorr sullenly.

"What tracks then were those I saw?" demanded the bishop.

"Your own, most likely, if you saw any."

But Elmys, the chief huntsman, now put in his word.

"He might have been forced from the wood a dozen times Lord Bishop, but that would not do, you would see the colour of him."

"What do you mean?" Vortipore exclaimed. "Speak out!"

"No," said Elmys slowly, "I cannot tell white from red. Ask Gurdney with the cat's eyes. He can see."

"The fact is, Lord Count," said Gorr, who saw that an explanation was due, "I always dread this part of the forest. Woodcraft and skill go for nothing in a region full of illusion and enchantment. I ask you, Elmys, if you

have not seen lights and heard sounds ;
nightly horrors which are not human ? "

The chief huntsman was constrained to
admit that it was so.

" Yes," continued Gorr, " it cannot be
denied that there is a spell on these woods.
As the stag leaped over the black brook
which runs westward to the Ouse, a misty
form rose from the stream and cast water
upon the beast; whereupon the colour became red, and the tines of the horns fewer.
The fact is—— "

But Gurdney with the cat's eyes, being
pushed forward, broke in—

" The fact is this man is a liar, probably
a traitor ; at least he has dealings with the
Saxons which you, Lord Count, would do
wisely to look into. We all know for what
crimes he was banished from the territory of
Anderida. As to the white hart, I saw
Gorr's beast early this morning."

" You never saw the white hart," cried
Gorr furiously.

" No," answered Gurdney, " but I saw all

that you saw, and more. He harboured last
night an old grey stag about a mile from the
spot where you broke your fast this morning.
More than an hour ago the stag was changed.
I did not see the misty form arise from the
brook, but I marked where the grey stag
pushed up an ordinary red one, which is now
somewhere in front of the hounds. In one
thing Gorr speaks the truth, this land is
full of delusions; so is every land where he
comes, and will be till his breath is shortened.
A little way to your right, Lord Count, is a
convenient tree, and for a halter——"

"You will not listen to this man. I am
your old and faithful——"

"I never heard of your faith," cried Madoc.
"As an exile you are liable to be hanged,
and if Gurdney can find a halter——"

"In my opinion," said the bishop, "as a
spiritual person, the best way to break the
enchantment is to hang Gorr on the en-
chanted ground; and for a halter——"

"Lord Count!" cried Gorr, "I am here
with your license, on your service."

"Aye," Vortipore answered, "to show me a white stag. Let me see it, and you are free to come and free to go."

"How can I, with all these in league to baffle me ? "

"I fear that you are a deceiver, Gorr," said the Count; "and though my heart inclines to mercy, justice demands that you should be scourged till you discover the truth. Strip him and tie him up ! "

This was done, and in Gorr's pouch they found two ornaments of Saxon workmanship, which did not dispose the men to gentleness, and his cries rang far through the forest."

Elmys promised that the stag they were after should be killed in half an hour; those who had led horses mounted them, and all took their appointed stations.

By the side of the Count stood Gurdney with the cat's eyes, holding the leash of Cavall, a noble Gallic hound thirty-two inches high, with rough coat, sharp muzzle, and eager eyes; the swiftest beast in Britain.

The air was chill ; where the sky could be

seen it was overcast with gloomy clouds
speeding rapidly over the openings of the
wood. Down below they felt little wind at
present, but the leaves rustled fitfully in the
increasing puffs which brought a drizzling
mist and made the gloomy forest alleys yet
more dim.

Beside the Count was a straight, dark
avenue, down which the wind blew and the
thin rain came and went. Disregarding all
the sounds in other directions, Cavall gazed,
bright-eyed, into the opening, now straining
at the leash, now shifting his feet impatiently.
Gurdney, with outstretched neck, looked in-
tently in the same line, and presently, with
a movement almost imperceptible, touched
the Count lightly on the knee. Vortipore
looked steadily over their heads, but at first
could make out nothing. Then he became
aware of a great hart, white as a summer
cloud, standing among the trees three hundred paces distant. Its head was turned
away and it seemed to scent something in
that direction. But as Vortipore shortened

his rein, and Gurdney slipped Cavall, it looked toward them, and vanished. The hound was out of sight almost as quickly, and Vortipore with a shrill hola followed.

The bishop and Etlym with the red sword galloped in the direction pointed out by Gurdney with such hounds as were at hand, and blew their horns to bring up the rest. Farinmail and a few others followed the sound, but got away so badly that they had no chance.

The stag at first made several attempts to go up the wind, but something he saw, heard, or scented always turned him back. These efforts and the holding nature of the ground gave Cavall such an advantage that they were abandoned, and the deer settled into a course at right angles with the current of air and soon came to the edge of the wood.

Vortipore took a diagonal line where the trees were scattered and the soil dry. He had occasional glimpses of pursuer and pursued, till at length emerging from under the boughs he had the delight of beholding the

great white hart, with antlers thrown back on
his shoulders, launch himself into the air over
a mass of thorn and bramble, and fly up the
short turf with a speed apparently not inferior
to that of Cavall, who was sixty yards behind
him. Up the long slope they raced all three,
until the increasing steepness of the ascent
forced them to make a slant along the hill-
side, when Vortipore saw the bishop, followed by Etlym, riding toward a gap in the
crest of the ridge through which instinct,
born of long experience, told him the chase
must go. But ever as they mounted higher,
the south-wester blew more fiercely, driving
thick fine rain like smoke across the upland,
hound and stag disappearing by degrees in
the cloud. Still the Count followed the slot,
which the sharp hoofs of the heavy hart im-
pressed deeply in the sward, and at length
reached the gap, where neither the bishop
nor Etlym could be seen. Here the marks
showed that the stag had turned to the westward, so that the ridge to the south was a
shelter from the violence of the increasing

gale. Presently the sharp yelp of a dog was
heard in front, and soon traces of blood
stained the grass. The Count followed the
tracks, every minute more slowly and wearily,
till on turning to the southward, the full concentrated fury of the tempest burst upon him,
and his tired horse wheeled away from it.
Pressing his thick felt hunting hat on his
head with one hand, he forced the animal
with rein and knee and spur to face the
storm, but still the horse swung round again
with his tail to the blast, and refused to meet
the stinging drops, mingled with hail, which
swept the height. All hope of slaying the
white hart was gone. Vortipore gave it up,
and sat gloomily gazing to leeward, cursing
with fierce oaths the horse, the deer, the
weather and himself.

As the clouds cleared a little, his face suddenly changed.

What he saw in that pool down below by
the edge of the wood none can tell. A blank
horror fixed his face; retracted lids and lips
showed lines of white teeth and white eye-
balls.

He was aroused by a clear voice above him, exclaiming—

"Welcome, Vortipore to Pen y Coit! Seventeen long years have we awaited your coming—seventeen years to the day; how short they seem now! We have waited, I and another. Do you know who that other is? You do. I see consciousness in that shudder. Again you would give her the head of the stag, the white hart of Pen y Coit. Or are you shivering from wet and cold? I will lead you to shelter, homely but hearty. An hour's riding will bring you to the hut of a charcoal-burner."

"Man or fiend," cried Vortipore, "I care not. Here our quarrel shall be finished— from this hill one of us goes down no more."

And drawing his hunting sword, he pushed his horse up to where the speaker stood. But he, a man clad in brown frock with leathern girdle, and bearing the staff and gourd of a pilgrim, flinched not a foot. He threw, or seemed to throw, something in the horse's nostrils as it approached, and the

animal stood as if rooted to the spot. Then
tossing back his hood, he fastened his
flashing eyes on the Count, and showing on
his shaved crown a long deep scar, exclaimed, "Fool! Can you kill men twice?
Am I not Renatus, he who was slain, come
again to repair the wrongs which you are not
weary of committing? How easily is the
mighty warrior disarmed! Come, we will go
down together."

With a twirl of his staff he struck the
sword from the Count's grasp, then taking
the bridle of the horse in his right hand he
led it down the southern side of the hill,
neither speaking again nor looking once
behind him.

Vortipore had lost, for a time, not only all
power of resistance, but even the capacity of
entertaining such an idea; he felt helpless in
the hands of the avengers.

What but the justice of Heaven could have
brought together himself and the being he
so justly dreaded at that spot on that day.
Absorbed in painful thought, unconscious

both where he was and whither going, he felt
a cold nose thrust into the hand which hung
disarmed by his knee. It was Cavall, who
having lost the deer, after getting several
wounds which would have been more serious
later in the year, now looked wistfully in his
master's face.

Vortipore loved dogs and horses because
they served his ends, but had no perception
that there were feelings common to man and
brute, through which a current of sympathy
might run. But looking down into the
beautiful honest eyes of the hound, his need
made him feel that there might be friendship
and language without articulate speech.

He was stooping from his saddle to caress
this friend in need, whose aid might extricate
him from an unpleasant position, when the
horse stopped at a hovel dimly seen in the
damp shade of the forest.

" Seventeen years," said the pilgrim turning
to Vortipore, " have changed the aspect of
harmless nature as well as the features of
wretches such as you and I. A welcome

to him who returns—there are who return not."

As he spoke the door opened. A woman, tall and graceful, stood within. Her dress, falling in straight scanty folds, was white; her head-dress, hiding her hair and passing under her chin, was white; her face was white and wan, corpse-like, but for the dark, deep-set eyes.

"See," the pilgrim said, "they have hunted the white hart of Pen y Coit."

She threw up her arms with a gesture of despair.

"Oh, they kill him!" she shrieked. "They strike with the sword on his bare head! They thrust him down! The waters are red with the blood of the innocent!"

With an exclamation of despair the Count turned away. Weird voices sounded in his ears as he sped through the dark wood, till his head struck an overhanging bough, and he fell on the leaves of vanished years.

CHAPTER II.

THE gale abated as the night wore away, but rain continued to fall heavily. The morning broke wet and cold in the camp where Farinmail and Madoc, with the rest of the party, had spent the night, and were preparing an organized search for the Count, the Bishop, and Etlym with the red sword. All the other stragglers either had come to the call of whoop and horn, or had found the camp fires during the night. With the earliest glimmer of light, Gurdney with the cat's eyes went away, and succeeded in tracking the stag and one horse to the gap of Pen y Coit ; beyond that point the traces were obscure. It was thought best to spread themselves in a long line, and sweep round the base of the hill in quest of their friends.

Several hours before noon, when they were ready to start, three horsemen were seen advancing slowly by the skirt of the wood; and Cavall, not much the worse for his hurts, came bounding toward them. Farinmail and Madoc rode forward and met the Count, conducted by the bishop and Etlym. Vortipore had been stunned, but the stooping attitude in which he rode, and the thickness of the petasus, or hunting hat, which he wore, saved him from serious injury; nevertheless his mind had received a shock, and he had eaten nothing for twenty-four hours.

The bishop and Etlym, when they gave up the chase, got the hounds together, and made their way to a sloping ground at the edge of the forest, where a number of large hollies afforded partial shelter. There Etlym dug a trench with his sword to carry off the water, and helped the bishop to build a hut of branches, which kept off the rain fairly enough. They kindled a fire before the entrance, divided the food they had with them, emptied the leathern bottle, put fresh logs on the embers, and slept serenely.

Before daylight the bishop's rest was disturbed by something wet and cold being thrust against his cheek, and a snuffling blast of air in his face ; but his conscience was easy, and his frame weary, he turned over to the other side and slept again.

Presently he felt himself lifted by the collar, his head swayed about for some time, and then dropped with a bump on the earth, while at the same moment a terrific howl made the leaves tremble. He woke, and became aware of two dreadful green eyes glaring at him out of the darkness.

It might be a wild beast, or it might be the devil, and to be prepared for either event he began, while he groped for his knife—

" Exorciso te in nomine——"

But before he got any farther, a short bark reassured him, and stretching out his hand he touched a rough head and fine muzzle

which he knew must belong to Cavall.   He
tried to make the hound lie down, for he was
full of sleep, and the big drops came with a
regular pour.   Cavall, however, was come on
business, and had no idea of neglecting it.
The bishop had a vague presentiment of
what was expected of him, for Pen y Coit was
a dangerous place for riding in such weather
as yesterday.

With a yawn and a shiver he woke Etlym
and went out, stirred the ashes and threw an
armful of brushwood on the fire.   The grey
light was growing in the east, near objects
were becoming obscurely distinguishable
through the falling rain ; a thrush began his
matins in the hollies ; a few trills from a robin
promised finer weather at hand ; then came
three or four sounding taps from a wood-
pecker's beak, and a yaffling laugh as he flew
away among the beeches.

As the bishop noted these things, Cavall
took a hand in his powerful jaws, and gently
pulled him towards the wood.

"Yes," he said, turning to Etlym, " I

guess what the beast means. Some one has met with an accident, probably the Count, and we must go to his assistance. But we must wait for more light, and meantime let us see what is left in the larder ; ' meat and mass never hinder work.' "

When they had emptied the valise and Etlym's pouch, and given the leathern bottle several expostulatory shakes, as if it might have refilled itself miraculously, like the widow's cruse, Etlym said—

" We may as well saddle the horses."

" I think not. The horses had a long day yesterday, and may have a long one to-day. Let them feed till we return."

They followed the hound on foot, chopping branches by the way to guide them on the backward track. An hour's brisk walking brought them to the spot where Vortipore lay beneath an oak, sleeping heavily. They roused him and set him on his steed, which grazed in a glade beyond, then led him to their hut, and afterwards, under the guidance of Cavall, to the other camp.

After meat and wine, Vortipore revived somewhat, the camp was broken up, and they started to return. Farinmail questioned the Count about his adventures, but got such curt, impatient answers, that he desisted from the attempt.

It was a dreary march, though the weather cleared after noon, and they kept to higher ground and straighter ways than had been selected by Gorr. Streams were running on all sides, damp places had become swamps, and swamps were extended into lakes. Even on the firmer ground everything was poached into black sludge by the trampling of nearly a hundred horses.

As the weary bespattered train dragged itself along, the bishop remarked to Farinmail—

" I cannot persuade myself that we have not just come out of the ark of Noah, the waters having recently retired from the earth."

" Pray where are the clean beasts ? " asked Farinmail.

Vortipore sent on for a fresh horse to meet him, and pushed forward, regardless of any one else, to Farinmail's disgust.

" In an expedition like this all should take the rough and smooth together. If one, and he the host, rides away to take care of himself, there is an end of the fellowship."

" The Count is more hurt than we think, perhaps," Etlym explained. " From what he said when we woke him, and his mutterings since, I suspect that he has seen some horror."

" The whole affair was ill-timed, ill-planned, ill-executed, and unlucky. Speaking of the execution, what became of Gorr ? "

" I do not know. Elmys, what did you do with Gorr ? "

" I did nothing," said Elmys. " I went after the red deer, before that luckless white one was found. Here, you fellow, what did you do with Gorr after he was scourged ? "

"We did nothing, master, we just let him alone."

" Let him alone, left him tied fast to that tree ? "

"Oh, he was tied fast enough," said the man coolly, "and nobody said anything about untying; shouldn't wonder if he's there still."

"Somebody is sure to find him," quoth Etlym carelessly.

"No," said Elmys the chief huntsman, "it is one of the most unfrequented parts of the forest."

"It would have been better to have hanged him outright," Farinmail remarked.

"He deserves the worst that can befall him," was Madoc's judgment, "but I would have reserved him for future examination, that he might disclose his motives; perhaps his confederates."

"I would have given him his viaticum," the bishop said, "and dispatched him with due care and solemnity."

"It was the cries of Gorr, Lords," Gurdney with the cat's eyes asserted, "that blanched the stag when he would otherwise have gone away up the wind. I could not hear them myself, but the stag did, as I judge from the direction in which his ears were pricked when I first saw him."

" Better have hanged him," Farinmail repeated, " best of all never have given ear to him. I foresee that we shall regret this senseless expedition."

" Nay," the bishop replied, " never regret a hunting match. At the best it is the crown and quintessence of happiness ; at the worst it is better than the best day spent other-wise."

" The claims of religion always reserved," laughed Comail.

" Be not irreverent, young man," the bishop retorted. " Things religious and things secular are of different orbs. They can no more be compared than the music of the spheres with a dish of surmullet."

The foulest way has an end if one trudge long enough. An hour before sunset, at two leagues * distance from Anderida, they came

---

* About 2·75 miles English. The .Gallic leuga (leuca in Domesday) contained 1500 Roman paces, each pace five Roman feet.

to the camp of the men of Gwent. It was situated on an eminence commanding the Roman road and the flats and marshes which extended in a westerly direction to the chalk hills. The foss and agger were complete on all four sides of the square, and men were busily interweaving the side branches of the sharpened stakes which formed the palisade.

While Farinmail wondered at the unusual precautions, Julius arrived with his train, and explained the reason of the work. He had set the men to work to give them something to do, that discipline might not be altogether relaxed. News had arrived in the afternoon, which caused him to push on the defences with all his energy.

"These works which surprise you, Lord Farinmail," he said, "are intended to prevent a surprise of more unpleasant nature."

"For two days," Farinmail replied, "almost every event has been a surprise, and every surprise an unpleasant one. Pray has the Count passed this way?"

"I have not seen him. I am but now come from the two other fortified camps we have established to watch the Cuckmare * river and the approaches from it."

"What! Are the Saxons stirring again already?" asked Farinmail.

"You shall hear. A mission from Ælle came this morning concerning the release of your prisoners, for whom I demanded on your behalf fifty pounds of silver, part of which is paid, and a portion of the captives dismissed. The escort sent with the ransomed Saxons brings reports from certain agents, which show that men are pouring in with such alacrity that Ælle's host is nearly as numerous as before his defeat. The levies include boys of sixteen and men between forty and sixty."

"Having beaten the fighting men," said Madoc, "the real strength of the foe, we shall not fear the old men and children."

* Probably a Celtic name; perhaps from Cwch, a concavity, and Marian, a strand. The river is remarkable for its tortuous course and winding shores.

"Where are our forces?" Julius answered. "When you are at leisure to count your own followers, Lord Madoc, do so. If out of four hundred and fifty you find forty-five in camp, I am in error."

Ælle cannot be very formidable yet," Farinmail said; "this is only the fourth day since we gave him a bloody defeat. Has he the magic caldron of Ierne in which the slain are revived?"

"He has better gifts than magic pretends to bestow. He has foresight and energy, which draw resources from earth and sea. He has wisdom to know how much may be done and undone in four days."

So saying the Praefect went to look after certain ships, some laden with corn, and others with salt from the salt-pans opposite to Vectis. From the mariners he learned that the whole Saxon fleet had disappeared from those parts; not a boat nor a man remained. There could be little doubt as to its destination.

"There he goes," exclaimed Madoc, looking after the Praefect; "the only capable man in his own conceit. He makes the worst of everything to exalt his own reputation in the amending of it."

But Farinmail, still resenting the Count's discourtesy, answered—

" Under some probable exaggeration there is at least this truth—that time has been wasted in a discreditable manner, and if you wish to secure the fruits of victory you must stretch out your hands. For myself, as this Count of yours seems to desire my aid no longer, I shall depart from him as soon as my arrangements are completed. If he have any message to Caradoc, my father, let it be brought to me by noon to-morrow at the latest."

" Lord Farinmail, we cannot suffer you to quit us in anger. We are not ungrateful. Any unintentional slight shall have ample apology and atonement."

" I measure your feelings toward myself by your conduct to the Lord Praefect. If the Count of the Saxon Shore would say anything to me, it must be said before noon to-morrow." And so, with a cold salute to Madoc, Farinmail turned away.

"When you have served our purpose," growled Madoc, as soon as the young chief was out of hearing, "you will probably be laid aside as better men have been and will be; but we cannot spare you yet." Then mounting a fresh horse, he hastened to the palace, resolved that on an issue of such vital importance there must be no ceremonious delay.

He found, however, that the Count was not to be disturbed. In vain he urged the absolute necessity of an interview; the chamberlain replied that the orders were too stringent to be disobeyed.

Foiled in this attempt, Madoc went in search of the bishop, whose powers of persuasion were notorious. The chamberlain was inexorable, and the cheerful ecclesiastic devoted himself to the task of mollifying Farinmail.

Vortipore meanwhile, in silence and in

solitude, passed in review the events of seventeen years. He could not think to any purpose, but the buzzing in his ears, and the curdling of twilight into darkness, fashioned themselves into sights and sounds, ghosts of evil words and evil deeds, which changed before his senses could apprehend their significance. Instead of sharp pangs he had an aching consciousness of impending punishment—a doom deserved and inevitable.

Celt and Saxon were closing for the death struggle, but he felt himself impotent to help or hinder. If any one thrust a sword into his hand he was ready to slay and be slain, but for the duties of a leader of men he was disabled.

Brooding over his sins with disordered brain, draining cup after cup of tasteless wine, he sat alone till night covered him.

CHAPTER III.

IT was late in the evening of the day after the hunting, that two men traversing the forest were arrested in their progress by a feeble groan, which seemed to come from a rising ground to their right.

The failing light could scarcely pierce the domes of thick foliage overhead, but enough found its way through openings here and there to show a dark object, which might be human, and seemed to cling about the base of a young tree.

With no weapons but pilgrims' staves, they went up to the spot in a way which proved that they feared neither thieves nor spirits. It was their function to deal with the latter, and as for robbers, they were in the state

described by Junius Juvenalis, whose verses
the elder of the two had studied in his un-
regenerate youth. Their scrips contained
nothing but morsels of black bread, and he
must have been poor indeed who could covet
their woollen frocks. The elder of the two
had a curious foreign water-gourd—these few
things and their lives were all they had to lose.

The dark mass proved to be a man, almost
dead, half hanging by the wrists to the side
branches, half supported by the ground and
the roots of the tree. The rain had soaked
the leathern thongs which bound him, so
that they stretched very much, the knots had
slipped up too tightly to be undone, and they
had no knife to cut them. The elder pilgrim,
Renatus, undertook to support the helpless
body in his arms, while the acolyte ran for
help. Renatus sighed to see the weals and
wounds on the bare back.

" Mitis Iesu ! " he cried, "another victim
of this man's cruelty—a persecuted saint, I
doubt not, stripped and scourged and left
to hang through such a night ! How long

O Lord, how long?" Then, after a pause,
while he shifted his hold to get the man in an
easier attitude and poured water between the
white lips, "Oh, that I had faith to turn
this water into wine. Wretch that I am, my
sins prevail! Mater misericordiae! plead
for me. But what am I, that a miracle should
be wrought through me?"

His arms and back ached sorely before the
acolyte returned with a couple of rough men,
who carried a piece of blackened sacking
fastened at the sides to two poles. They cut
the thongs from the man's wrists and ankles,
and laying him on the sacking, face down-
ward, bore him to the hut whither Vortipore
had been led the evening before. The same
tall, ghost-like woman opened the door, to
whom Renatus spoke—

"Sister, we bring you a suffering brother
—a lamb torn by the wolf who has destroyed
so many, and now has tortured this holy man,
I venture to say, for refusing compliance."

"Lamb!" said one of the charcoal-burners,
who had been examining the face by the

light of a splinter of pine. "Holy man! this is that cowardly villain Gorr, who stole mother Modron's sheep, and shot her son, who accused him of it, in the back; luckily the arrow glanced and did not kill him."

"Well," said Renatus, "he is wounded, naked, wanting all things; we will succour him for Christ's sake."

"Take care, then," the father of the first speaker growled; "if you do him a good turn he always requites it with an evil one."

"Men," answered Renatus, "how often must I teach you that love is stronger than malice? What were you, what was I, what are we now? Sinners, whom God teaches to love and help sinners as He loves and helps us."

"It is not for us to set ourselves against you, who are wise and good, but we were never like this fellow. He is a coward, a traitor, true to no man. A slimy eel, who slips away in the mud. Ill luck is his who trusts him."

"The worse he is, the more need to show

him what is good. Let us be careful so to behave ourselves that he may see the beauty of virtue and religion, what peace and happiness they bring."

" Peace and happiness," sighed the lady, "not till grass and innocent flowers grow over this corrupt flesh."

By this time she had heated water, and mixing wine with it, she raised Gorr's head and made him drink. He opened his eyes to steal a furtive glance around. The warmth recalled his wandering spirits, and they fed him with bread soaked in milk.

Then she applied a poultice of mallow leaves to his back, after which they laid him on a low bed and bid him sleep.

The charcoal-burners, father and son, went to their couch of fir branches, in an adjoining hut, but Renatus, and she whom he had addressed as sister, exercised themselves in offices of devotion far into the night.

Before he left, Renatus threw a handful of twigs on the dying fire, and as they burned up, spoke—

"You say truly, peace and happiness are not for us on this side of the grave. Do I not see in your heart even now a restless craving, cherished and unconfessed."

"I strive against it." Then with a sob that shook her wasted form, she cried—

"Oh thou who art thyself a mother, pity me, pity me!"

"She hears you," said Renatus, solemnly. "Her ears cannot be closed to such a call. With her help and blessing I may be able to gratify your desire. God be with you."

She barred the door behind him, and also that leading to the out-house where Gorr lay, then casting herself on the earth, she prayed with words and inarticulate sounds, heaping ashes on her head. This seemed inadequate to express her grief. Hastily removing the dress and hair shirt from her shoulders, she seized a short-handled knotted scourge, and lashed herself fiercely till blood oozed from the skin. Then grovelling again on the ground, she wept till kindly sleep overpowered her.

Smith, who with bandaged head and whitened face personated a wounded Gesith, had recovered apace, and managed to get about with the help of a stick. He was usually to be found near the forge of his friend the cutler, with whom he exchanged trade secrets. The forge commanded a view of the postern, but there was another point of even more importance in his eyes, namely, the place where Ostrythe would probably escape from the palace. Not that it seemed very likely that flight would be attempted, but Smith would have grieved that it should be accomplished without his assistance, and therefore kept in the way. In a secret nook of his heart he entertained a serene admiration for Ostrythe, tempered with knowledge of his own desert. To him, as to many of his tribe, it was inconceivable that anything could be too good for him, and though the lady was a king's daughter and promised to another man, he had a chaotic feeling not developed in express thought that the destinies would be careful not to leave him discontented. Such a sentiment, combined with a pushing, persevering temperament often carries men to heights far beyond their merit and capacity, as their fellows judge.

Smith's unexpressed devotion to his own interest embodied in Ostrythe, led him to make a friend of Rhys, the back of whose house overlooked the lane he desired to watch, while the front was in the same street as the cutler's forge.

Rhys had returned home, got rid of all his household, except one old woman, and discontinued his business. He went about mostly in the dark, addressed no one, and answered questions in a dull, distraught manner. Smith noticed his malcontent air and ascertained from sympathizing neighbours the cause of it.

He took occasion to do Rhys sundry small services, for which he received curt and grudging thanks.

" A stranger," Smith said on one of these occasions, " a stranger might suppose, from the looks of us two, that you were the

prisoner and I the free man.   Cheer up, man,
and have a joyous look as of old ! "

" There   is   a   worse   lot   than   captivity,"
Rhys replied.

" Yes ; but to every ill there is a remedy.
The proverb says, ' To the weary, slumber ;
to   the   hungry,   food ;   to   the   wronged,
revenge.' "

" That is a good proverb," said Rhys, and
went into his house.

Some time afterwards, as Smith was passing, Rhys called to him—

" Will you come in, friend, and taste my
wine ? "

Smith, nothing loth, soon had a horn of
generous wine in his hand.

" I am not by nature the surly companion
I seem now," Rhys continued ; " I love to be
merry among my fellows, but of late——"

" Ay, ay ! Men say you have had grievous
wrong."

" Men say ! Do they speak of it in the
streets ? "

" That they do. How else should I hear
of it ? " replied Smith.

"What do they say?" inquired Rhys, fiercely.

"They whisper, 'It's not like stout Rhys to be so quiet.'"

"I am not myself," said Rhys sadly; "I am not the same man since that night. When I try to plan my revenge, when I would collect my thoughts, they buzz in my head, hither, thither, like a swarm of bees—bees without honey, without sting."

"I would help you," said Smith, "if I knew how."

"If I had a friend to stand by me when my head swims, to steady me, I could do something. I am apt enough to devise, but when I set about doing, my eyes are clouded, and everything turns. You could help me better perhaps than one of our own people, for no one would suspect you of any design."

"I will do what I can. First of all, tell me what are your customs, by what means do you punish the wrong-doer?"

"By the law. But law is of no avail in this case. The Praefect will do justice as far

as he can see, but this is beyond his scope.
What would you do ?"

"Well," said Smith, filling his horn and
settling himself for a comfortable exposition,
"other folks have ways of their own, which
may be better than ours, or may be worse, I
won't say. We need not go into the questions of land or money, which the moots
decide; nor into those of maiming, blood-
shedding, and murder, though we might
profitably do so. This is a case of deadly
wrong, for which you say the law affords no
redress. Our custom is so simple and convenient to all concerned that I never heard a
complaint of its working. We gather kinsfolk
and friends, go to the offender's house and
burn it; having previously made sure that he
is inside. Those of his family who have
taken no part——"

"Oh, curse the family!" ejaculated Rhys.

"No, no! We do not punish the innocent
with the guilty. Wife and children, slaves
and strangers, are to come forth, unless they
choose to remain within. If they wish to

stay they are allowed to do so, for we are a free people and respect the rights of others while we vindicate our own."

" Burn the house and him in it," cried Rhys, banging his fist on the table ; "that's the plan, and the other rats may shift as they can ; I shall look after him. The first thing to be done is to examine the house and to know perfectly all the passages, stairs, and means of escape."

" Very good ; and now how to get in ? "

" Oh," said Rhys, "with good clothes and a confident bearing, one may go almost anywhere without question."

In pursuance of this plan, they spent the day in exploring all parts of the palace to which they could gain access, especially the prince's quarters, and at night scaled the wall and made themselves familiar with the terraces.

Only the edge of the storm which swept the downs and part of the forest, had touched Anderida. It reached the city later and blew less furiously. The following day was gloomy and damp, and the dreary skies reflected themselves in Bronwen's mood. She assuaged the irritation of her soul by tormenting every living thing that came in her way; slaves, dependants, and pets had a hard time. Ostrythe missed the home work, the spinning, the oversight of the maidens, the housewifely duties of a Saxon lady, and spent most of her time on the tower from which she had marked the flight of Sæfugl.

It was late when they heard of the Count's return, and of his refusal to see any one. With a feeling of relief that the day was over, they betook themselves to their lofty bed.

About midnight Ostrythe, weary of tossing sleeplessly from side to side, rose quietly, and without disturbing Bronwen, descended the steps and dressed herself. Then she stepped over the two girls who were stretched in slumber across the doorway, with a rushlight burning in a vessel of bronze beside them; and raising the curtain, entered the room beyond. The perfumes, which Bronwen loved, stifled her; she opened a window latticed with slender, interwoven strips of willow, and drank in the dank sea-smelling night breeze. The window looked on the same terrace as did those of the chamber she first occupied, and was nearer to the spot which she had chosen for her descent into the street. The fresh, free air awakened in her a yearning for freedom and home, and she leaned out studying the relative positions of objects showing darker against the darkness.

Then she reflected that Æscwine would soon return, perhaps to-morrow, and release her without any risk incurred. Bronwen had made her understand that there were dangers for a woman in the streets of the city, dangers which the simple Saxon but vaguely apprehended—from which she shrank with a fear which the beasts of the forests could not inspire.

She put down her hand to the hunting greaves she still wore, and felt Æscwine's dagger, with a hope that no necessity for its use would arise.

While she thus pondered whether to escape or to stay, this scale now declining and now that, a puff of wind, as from an opened door, caused her to look round.

The three-beaked lamp, which hung untrimmed from the ceiling, gave a smoky light, and wavering shadows filled the room.

A man advanced unsteadily, supporting himself on any piece of furniture which came to his hand, and Ostrythe with some difficulty recognised him as Vortipore. The strong wine which the Count took to dispel the gloom of his spirits had done its work ; remorse had vanished, and with it had flown the volatile goddess, Discretion, who spreads her wings at the approach of wine, fear, or passion. He remembered the maid with the broom-flower hair, and resolved to honour her with a visit.

His tongue was as titubant as his gait ; moreover he spoke Latin, a language which Ostrythe did not understand, but she could not mistake the meaning conveyed by his eyes and his insolent gestures. She sternly bid him stand back, drawing at the same time her dagger from its sheath. He advanced, protesting his unchangeable love. They were not two yards apart; in another moment the broad, sharp blade would have been among the great veins of the Count's throat, when a cry was heard from the door of the sleeping-room. Vortipore turned and saw, framed in the doorway, a tall, slender female figure in a white dress which fell in straight scanty folds to her feet. Her head-dress was white, her face was white, with large dark eyes.

In horror he averted his face, stretched his hands, palms outward, toward the vision, and losing his balance, fell drunkenly on his face. Bronwen, who had been aroused by the sound of the voices, sprang to her father's side with a shriek which brought to her aid the slave girls, as well as the two attendants with torches whom the Count had left outside.

In the confusion Ostrythe slipped unseen on to the terrace. Angry and wondering at what she had witnessed, she determined to quit at once this wretched den. She paused in the darkness to ascertain her course, and to recall the directions given by Æscwine. Then, groping her way to the wall, she found the broken battlement just above the heap of rubbish, knelt on the broad string-course outside, and grasping a decayed iron cramp dropped lightly to the earth.

She sped along the street which led to the intervallum and, turning the corner sharply, ran against brother John, who, with Eleutherius the scribe, was on his way to the bedside of a dying man. John well nigh dropped the taper and pyx which he carried, and burned his fingers with scalding wax.

The sudden apparition of a woman at such an hour, in such a place, when they were on such an errand, naturally suggested to the brethren the idea of the old enemy and his wily snares. They crossed themselves hastily, and John began an exorcism, but Eleutherius, who was of a more constant temper, seeing that Ostrythe was disposed to escape, laid hold of her garment, gaining the courage which ebbed from her.

" Touch her not," cried John, "it is a spirit of evil ! "

"It is no spirit, brother, but a woman—solid flesh ; and I would fain know what she does here at this time of night.

Saying this, Eleutherius grasped John's hand and turned it so that the taper shed its light on Ostrythe's face.

" Brother, brother ! you know not their arts. Fly, escape ! Remember the capitulum, ' De oculis in mulierem non figendis !' Think of the words of Jeronimus, ' Janua diaboli, via iniquitatis, nocivumque genus femina ; fugias igitur——"

" Brother," answered Eleutherius impatiently, "your fears are misplaced. This person may be a minister of Satan, as all who do evil are, but she is one to be dealt with by the Praefect, though I must say her aspect is not ungracious."

" Taken in her net, caught by her charms —alas !—alas ! "

" And you," answered Eleutherius, " quid judicas fratrem tuum ? "

But John raised a reproving hand, and said sorrowfully—

" ' Considero vecordem juvenem qui transit per plateam juxta angulum '—at the corner. Mark the wise man's words."

" Vecors ! " cried Eleutherius. " Not so foolish as you."

" ' In noctis tenebris et caligine ; et ecce occurrit illi mulier.' "

" Occurrit mihi ! Slanderer ! " said Eleutherius with increasing wrath. " Mihi ! Why, she ran against you ! "

" ' Apprehensumque deosculatur,' " John proceeded calmly.

" This is too much. Your words are as false as they are foul."

But Ostrythe took the opportunity to elude the disputants ; and as Eleutherius turned to observe the last gleam of her dress vanishing in the obscurity, John struck in again—

" Statim sequitur eam quasi bos——"

" Spare your breath, I pray," Eleutherius

broke in. " While you have been occupying the time with visionary sins and sinners, the real offender, it may be, has escaped. But for your garrulity I would have known her errand."

" Her errand I can tell you," said John meekly. " It is to stir up the evil which lies at the bottom of men's hearts, to excite the lusts of the flesh in men vowed to holiness and self-denial, to move strife between brethren." Then, after a pause, " If I have wronged or offended thee, brother, I crave forgiveness. Let us think of our own errand."

" Let us do so," responded Eleutherius. " I have been deficient in respect to you, my elder, also ireful, and it may be light-minded. I have sinned. Ab irâ et superbiâ et oblectamentis carnis, libera me Domine."

And the good men, mindful of the Host they carried, went on their way in silence and with bowed heads.

But Ostrythe, with her hand on the city wall, stumbled along till the light from the guard-chamber streamed across the intervallum; and by the door she saw a man whom, from his size, she supposed to be Smith. As she drew nearer the supposition became certainty; and with footfalls as light as a cat's, she crept into the recess of the postern and laid her hand on his arm, saying—

"Ælle the King—I have the keys, and will leave them in the doors."

Smith's nerve would not have failed him amid the ruins of a shattered globe. He raised his growling voice, and blocked the door of the guard-room with his big body, effectually covering Ostrythe's movements as she pushed in the key and brought into play the studs which released the latches, and then turned the door on the bronze pegs which served as hinges. She drew her dagger and cut the thong that tied the keys together, passed through the door and closed it. Smith sidled quietly to the key, and muttered as he pocketed it—

"A cool lass and a clever one, just fit for me; and what an arm!"

Ostrythe stood on the dark sea-bank, beneath the rugged, lichen-hung thorn which had sheltered Ent's coracle. It was the night of the new moon, two hours and a half after high water. The trees on the opposite shore were invisible ; but the angry sound of the wind-driven sea as it met the tide on the roaring bar was loud in the lonely stillness. The spring ebb, reinforced by late rains, rushed by her feet with glimmering, gurgling swirl, and unshapen, uncanny objects hurried past.

Ostrythe was daunted by the prospect, as well she might be. Should she return ? Smith could conduct her to Julius, who would surely protect her. On the other hand, things seldom turn out so bad as they look. She hated to give up an enterprise once begun.

Hastily she unfastened her girdle, pulled off the upper and under tunics, which, with greaves and sandals, formed her whole attire, rolled them tightly and bound them on her head with the belt. The water crept over her feet, stole through the lacing of the greaves, and rose above one knee. She held back the other foot. It was not yet too late.

Out of the night and the silence came a wild cry, followed by violent and continued knocking. A light blazed out on the summit of the highest tower of the palace, casting a lurid glow around.

Ostrythe threw herself forward, and was swept away by the eager waters.

CHAPTER IV.

THE gale that swayed the woods and drove the mist and rain on Pen y Coit, caught the Saxon fleet in the Channel on its way to Wlencing harbour. They had been cruising to the westward of Vectis, stretched in a long line a few miles from the coast, enforcing their religious principle that all things belong rightly to those who can take and keep them. The summons of Ælle found the ships so widely dispersed that in spite of all efforts they reached the western side of Selsea only on the morning of the third day after the fatal fight on the downs. The flood tide inshore was spent, and they stood out to sea ten miles, to catch the offing tide, but the long war ships towed six heavy deep merchant vessels they had captured, which much impeded their progress.

About four hours after noon the south-wester blew strongly, the oars were laid in, and a mast was stepped forward on which a squaresail was hoisted, and each ship ran dead before the wind. The war ships were all built on the same plan, with slight differences of detail. They were about seventy-five feet long, ten to eleven in width, and drew about four and a half feet of water, with a flat floor. They pulled fifteen oars on each side, and had a short half-deck at either end.

Cymen, the Ætheling, was on the after-deck of the leading ship, his long hair, cut squarely over the brow, and his thick moustache, dripping with rain and spray. He stood between the two steersmen, his left hand grasping the staff from which streamed shoreward the ensign of the white dragon. Some averred that the figure on a red ground was a white horse, and cited ancient authorities. But a majority of the seamen held that, whereas it was not at all like a white horse which they had seen, it might be very like a white dragon which they had not seen. Whichever it were it answered its end; seldom failing to guide its followers to victory.

The spin-drift flew from the wave crests as the tawny, foam-laced seas came hissing after the ships, heaving and changing shape as they came. The steersmen dipped their oars with an accordant sweep as the swelling mass reached the ship, and the wave lifted the stern and melted from beneath it with an easy motion. Shading his eyes from the sharp drops with his right hand, the Ætheling strained his keen sight, trying to pick up his marks for the harbour mouth. They were within half a mile of the sandy spit, where the surf broke in long lines of white, before he could distinguish the timber structure which served as a beacon.

Then, as he raised his hand, a man beside him made an unearthly roaring on a horn, a signal at which every vessel lowered its sail

and fell into line behind the admiral. The
sea was heavy at the entrance of the harbour
formed by the expansion of the river behind
the spit of sand, the long ships took in much
water, and one of the merchant craft went
ashore. They were built to take the ground,
and of most solid construction. This vessel,
of sixty tons burden, sixty-five feet in length,
with fourteen feet beam, had timbers
eighteen inches deep by eight in thickness.
The tide had begun to flow, and she was got
off without much damage, beyond the loss
of some of the moss with which her seams
were caulked.

Ælle rejoiced at the arrival of the fleet
which was an accession to his force of fourteen hundred and fifty men of the toughest
fighting quality. Cissa had come in with
about eighteen hundred, many of them too
young or too old for severe work. There
were two thousand two hundred who escaped
unhurt from the battle, and three ships had
arrived from old Saxony with at least a
hundred men in each. The wounds were

healing apace, many of the less severely hurt were already trying if they could endure the weight and pressure of their armour.

The injuries these men received were cured as speedily and with as little inconvenience as those of wild animals, and for the same reasons. The weak and sickly fell a prey to the hardships of their lot before they reached maturity, only the strong and hardy transmitted their blood to posterity. Hating walled towns, where numbers are pent up in their own fetor, they lived a simple, natural life in the free air of fields or woods.

Ælle consulted with the wise men, whom he bent to his will. He put matters before them in such a shape that they, having full confidence in him, usually decided as he wished.

He told the Witan of the weakness and security of the Welsh, and proposed an immediate attack on their position, while the fleet went to blockade Anderida, and to make a diversion if fit occasion should arise,

The Council assented to both these measures, and Cymen sailed with the next afternoon's flood, and before dark was off the beach where Sæfugl lay. Eleven war ships and the six merchant vessels were put ashore in the soft mud, while two of the long swift craft kept afloat to watch the entrance to the harbour. The crews of the other vessels landed, lighted fires, which were invisible from Anderida through the high, thick woods, posted sentinels, supped, and went to sleep.

Some of the ship captains visited the outposts while Cymen and the others discussed plans for the morrow, little dreaming that at two furlongs distance the daughter of Ælle was in peril of her life.

Ostrythe swam strongly and steadily, sometimes holding her own, sometimes whirled away like a straw by a local current. She guided her course by the direction of the stream, and by the roar of the surf which seemed every instant to come nearer and louder. It was a terrible distance to the farther shore; perhaps in the darkness she did not take the best line across; perhaps she did not husband her strength. Every stroke was shorter than the last, her feet sank lower and lower, and the burden on her head became heavier. Still she struggled on, for to turn on her back and rest was to be swept among the waves of the bar; but she felt that she could not hold out long. Then a chill came over her; it was not the fear of death, but a horror of being cast naked and unseemly on the shore; if she could but loose her dress and wrap it about her, she thought she could drown contented.

She was not to be drowned—of course not. Eóstre, kindly goddess of spring, or some beneficent power, sent a pine log within her reach, over the middle of which she threw her tired arms. Resting and regaining breath and strength, she found that she was close to the wished-for bank, though near the point, and was able to discern the black woods from the clouds, which were now less dense and dark. She was caught in a back eddy, and the objects on shore sailed in a direction contrary to their previous unrelenting course. Her feet touched the shore, she waded to land, and fell exhausted on the shingle. As she lay the sound of voices reached her. Starting up she loosed the bundle from her head, squeezed the water from her hair, and brushed the drops from her skin, whose dangerous splendour was promptly eclipsed by the safer grey of her garments.

She stole round by the bushes, and beheld instead of Sæfugl a crowd of masts against the sky, and a score of fires smoking. It might be the Saxon fleet come to assail the Welsh, it might be a squadron of sea-rovers to whom nothing comes amiss.

While she doubted, two men laid hands on her. She was safe, and soon told her adventures to her brother. Then, after food and wine, she slept on a bed of leaves wrapped in Cymen's sea cloak.

The next morning the Ætheling ordered Sæfugl to be got ready to take Ostrythe to Wlencing, but first he examined her closely about the defences of Anderida. He was dissatisfied with the position he held. Wlencing had a place of importance which would bear his name to future generations. The camp near the ruins of Regnum was already becoming permanent with the name of Cissan-ceaster; but he, the eldest brother, had nothing to perpetuate his fame but the barren shore of Cymenes-ora, where they landed fourteen years ago. He would distinguish himself by some exploit more glorious than the capture of a few ships, whether equipped for war or trade.

How if he were to fulfil his father's wishes as to a diversion by storming the city out of hand. His skippers to whom he propounded the notion were delighted. They loved their sturdy leader and were jealous of his honour and of their own. The fleet had had no fighting of late; the land force on the contrary had come in for a good beating with a glorious list of killed and wounded, which was the next best thing to a bloody victory. How extremely pleasant it would be to take the city before the others came up, from under the noses of their brethren as it were ; and then not to be proud, not to give themselves airs, but to speak of it as a thing as natural as taking a drink for men who had not obscured their faculties by too much digging of the earth. It was an excellent notion, no one could doubt that, and the only point remaining for consideration was —how to get in. The walls were high and apparently thick, and there seemed little chance of using fire except at the gates.

So Cymen sat with Ostrythe on the bank looking towards the city, and above the grey misty woods on their right the sky was primrose, and pale pink and green, with a thin purplish cloud. It was nearly low water : a wasted stream crept between broad sloping shores of shining mud, out of which stuck a ragged bough hung with fringes of green weed, and near it a sheep, swollen and foul, lay half buried in the slime. Ostrythe shuddered and turned away.

She showed the Ætheling the postern by

which she escaped, and the tall tower of the palace whence came the sudden clamour and flame which startled her.

"It was a beacon," Cymen told her. "I saw two others on the hills west away there. The old man is rummaging their holds."

"And you want to rummage before him."

"Yes. So tell me all about the great gates. They are wooden?"

"Yes; and prodigiously thick and heavy. They are two-fold, and shut against the arch above and against stonework below. Through these men pass into a chamber in the thickness of the wall, closed on the city side by a pair of gates like the first."

"So we must provide firewood to burn both sets of gates."

"Then close behind the outer gate Æsc-wine showed me the place where a huge iron grating slides down. Cat—cata—cataracta, I think they call it. They drop this when the outer gate is forced, and pour hot sand and boiling oil and melted lead, and such like matters, on the men they have caught inside.

I saw the holes they pour through; it made my skin creep. Then they lift the grating, and if any more like to enter the trap they can."

"Now by Tiw the one-handed, a brave device," growled the Ætheling. "I should like to catch the inventors in that trap; a little burning pitch might be an improvement to the dish. After all we must do it with ladders; men don't like to be smothered in a hole like a nest of honey-bees. By him who put his hand in the jaws of the wolf, it is a good deed to exterminate these cunning cowards."

"Do you know, brother, I have heard these people call us stupid giants, who not having wit to make things for ourselves, take advantage of our size and strength to rob others."

"That is nonsense," said Cymen; "those who are bigger than ourselves are giants, those who are less, dwarfs; words have no meaning else. When men fight fairly, foot to foot, and Shieldmays hover around choos-

ing the brightest and bravest for the immortal
banquet, the gods look down with pride on
their children ; but the All-Father is grieved
when guile and fox-like craft prevail over
manly open strength and courage."

"That is true," said Ostrythe, "but I cannot help being sorry for these men, who
understand and make so many beautiful
things ; things we do not want—which we
cannot even keep."

"Men are better without such things—
they ruin good customs. Farewell, sister,
Sæfugl is ready. Say nothing of our plan
to the father. I am glad I sent men early
to cut sticks for the ladders."

Many hands make light work. The seamen wrought with a will. Some cut young
ash trees in the high wood, where they were
drawn up tall and straight, some dug a saw-
pit to cut the trees, many chopped rungs and
pegs, and one old sailor calculated with two
sticks and a cord, what length the ladders
should be to reach from a ship's deck to the
top of the wall.

The ships were lashed together in couples, and a platform established across their bows on which a pair of ladders worked on a kind of roller. A beam connected the mast-heads of the united ships, and a tackle from the beam raised or lowered the ladders. These were made of three split ashpoles with two sets of rungs, the rungs wide enough for two men to mount abreast on each. There were six pairs of vessels, each pair capable of putting four men on the wall at once.

A spot was indicated where the galleys could be hauled close to the wall, and slack water about two hours after sunset was chosen for the attack. "For," said a thoughtful skipper, "we know not whether it is a good place for ships to lie. The half hour's slack will give time for two things—to take the town and to haul the ships off afterwards. The ships will be afloat on this beach an hour before the slack, which will be enough to allow for getting into line and rowing easily in."

Their deliberations were interrupted by a

frightful yelling from the city; they asked themselves what it could mean.

" I hope," said Cymen, " that the old man has not forestalled us."

" No, no," cried several; "those are not voices of men and women ; it is the squealing of pigs or of cart-wheels."

" Perhaps," said a huge fellow, who even among the large-framed Saxons was nick-named Mucel, the big, "perhaps they are killing the boar, Sæhrimnir for those who shall sup with Woden to-night."

Men looked at each other. They knew that by this unlucky speech Mucel had fore-told his own destiny.

Just then the hideous screaming from the city made itself heard with increased inten-sity, and ceased suddenly with a shock ; a rushing sound was heard, a large white ball came crashing through the branches, breaking . and being broken. Men came running from the side next to the city telling how a gigantic arm as long as the city wall was high, had risen swiftly, and brandishing a sling of proportionate size, had discharged the ball. Some of the Saxons knew all about these engines, but most clung to diabolical agency.

Seven men were killed or seriously hurt by the missile. Many other balls fell, some on the land doing more or less damage, some in the sea, whereat the Saxons laughed. Julius was getting the range of his engines.

Cymen did not fail to point out to his followers that the nearer a man is to these engines the less risk he runs, and exhorted them ever to stand up for close quarters and fair fighting.

At the appointed time the vessels were ready, with ladders shipped, and ranged themselves in double line ; the first was to place itself as close to the wall as it could, then the oars being laid in, the ships of the second row were to be warped into the intervals between them ; the ladders would thus be near together and the assault concentrated.

They pulled slowly in, using the oars on

the disengaged side of each ship, directing
their course by the two towers between which
the attack was to be made, and carefully
keeping line and distance.

When they had rowed about a furlong, a
light was shown by a man on the shore, who
had a line of bearing taken with two trees.
This was a signal to Julius, and the engines
in the city were discharged. Two lighted
brands came whirling through the twilight
heaven, each attached to a ball of sandstone
twenty inches in diameter. The Saxons bent
their backs to the oars, hoping to get inside
their range. Down came the balls with
swifter and swifter revolution; one plunged
into the sea between the lines, dashing the
water in the men's faces; the other struck
one of the vessels amidships. The boat
heeled over as the stone, weighing more than
seven hundred and fifty pounds, tore through
platform, floors, and planking, making a
terrible hole. The sea poured in, she sank
deeper and deeper, till the tall ladder, toppling
over, dragged the twin barks to the bottom.

Several men were killed by the shot, several were dragged down in the wreck, the rest swam or clung to floating oars or planks till they were picked up.

Before the squadron recovered from its confusion, two more of the stones fell among them, carrying away the top of a ladder and breaking some oars. The lines were reformed, and advanced steadily toward the city, the tide helping them. At forty fathoms from the bank they let go anchors to warp off by, and were soon imbedded in the mud at the foot of the massive bulwark.

Cymen's signalman sounded his horn, the ladders were lowered and up the stormers went, each holding his shield over his head to ward off the stones and darts which came pelting from above. But when the foremost reached the summit, a fresh device of the crafty foe baffled them. Anticipating the point of attack, Julius had slung a framework of timber over the parapet and nine feet below it ; against this the ladders rested, and a wide gulf interposed itself between the tops

of the ladders and the wall. Cymen shouted
for men to clamber on to the frame and cut
it away, but as it was obvious to the most
obtuse that whoever performed this feat must
fall with the framework, no one thought himself in a position to get on the timber, but
urged his neighbour with much vehemence to
obey the command of the Ætheling.

Seeing this, Cymen hung his shield over
his shoulder, let his sword swing from his
wrist by the lanyard, climbed down the
underside of the ladder, and seating himself
on one of the timbers, began sawing at the
ropes which sustained it. The men gave a
deep growl of approbation and followed his
example in such numbers that the fabric
would have broken down under their weight
if the archers on the flanking towers had not
shot most of them.

Mucel was one of the topmost men on
another ladder, where his bulk loomed giant-
like against the sky. For a moment he
poised himself, then with wonderful lightness
for a man of his size and in full armour, he

sprang on to the wall. Striking with boss of buckler and pommel of sword, he cleared a space, other Saxons following with various results. Eight men he had hammered down, and the crowd of Britons cowered together from the sweep of his terrible arm.

Through the shrinking crowd a champion came, bigger - boned, longer - armed than Mucel himself, though of lower stature. It was Bael, bare-headed, bare-footed, with no body armour but his greasy leathern shirt, his fierce little eyes, wary and unwinking, his movements quick and ready as those of a wild beast.

The temper of the Saxon's sword was not good enough to bite on rhinoceros hide, and the weapon glanced from the sloped' shield. Instead of striking at the head, Bael tapped his antagonist with the back of his axe on that most tender spot inside the knee. For a moment the joint relaxed, the left arm dropped its guard, and the bronze blade sank deeply into the giant's brain. The Britons rushed in with a shout as he fell, and cut down the few who had followed their doomed comrade.

Julius meantime, from one of the flanking towers, watched with grim satisfaction the progress of affairs. The framework of timber was ready to fall, the ladders were crowded with armed men four abreast, and as soon as any fell, others pressed eagerly into the vacant places.

" Take good aim !" cried Julius. " Work the machines quickly, they will not be much longer in our power !"

The machines rattled, the missiles hissed through the darkening air; dead and wounded dropped like gorged leeches, heaped as the sands running through an hour-glass.

Holding on to the last ropes Cymen and several others divided them below their hands, hoping to retain their grip, but the jerk of the cords, suddenly released from the strain, was too great, and all lost their hold as the structure fell.

With a far more fearful crash the four ladders, each bending under the weight of

twelve tons of men, swayed down upon the
wall, struck the parapet, curved inward and
broke in pieces, hurling the whole mass of
the assailants in a horrible heap at the foot
of the rampart. Those above ceased not to
fling down beams and stones, boiling water,
burning pitch, with frantic cries and imprecations on the defeated sea-kings, who had
harassed them so cruelly and so long.

The ships were hauled off a short distance
to be beyond the reach of fire-balls, as well
as to avoid the risk of being left by the tide.

With the wreck of the ladders, and planks
from the platforms which united the vessels,
a sort of raft-bridge was constructed, and the
wounded crawled, or were helped or carried
on board.

The Ætheling was found stunned and
bruised, but with unbroken bones, among the
timbers of the fallen frame, part of which had
in some degree shielded him from blows and
pressure.

At length, when not the wounded only, but
also a considerable proportion of the dead

were in the ships, the Saxons sullenly rowed away into the darkness, having lost one-third of their force.

Anderida had sustained the first assault, and her citizens rested in trembling safety behind their Roman wall.

CHAPTER V.

GREAT was the consternation in the city when perils of war became evident to the senses, when the masts of the hostile fleet could be seen from one of the towers and strident voices of engines stirred the imagination of the most apathetic.

With many men, danger whose distance requires miles or years for its measurement, is no danger at all as far as fore-arming is concerned. Unceasingly, insensibly, the interval of space or time wastes away while they saunter unheeding, till with startled eyes they see the monster within springing distance, and enumerate in the multiplying speculum of fear the terrible teeth and claws.

The city guard, and many of the Roman party, were men not to be easily thrown off their balance by any hazard, but to the mass of the people it was but a step from assault to capture, and not so far from thence to destruction.

Julius, who had long foreseen the inevitable siege—inevitable from the passion and folly of those who should keep the foe from the wall—had made what preparations he could to meet it. Military engines of various kinds had been repaired, and new ones constructed, missiles of all sorts were accumulated, and the food magazines replenished. Sunken ships and other devices guarded the long bridge on the seaward side, and waterways leading to the interior were obstructed.

He was ready to repel the Saxon fleet, whose very rashness might have helped them against a careless enemy.

The beacons on the night of Ostrythe's escape announced that Saxon camp fires were visible from the forts on the downs. Ælle had not thought fit to risk another attack on a fortified position, and seemed disposed to content himself for the present with settling the territory which was abandoned to him, and with strengthening his frontier on the Cuckmare river. Victory could scarcely have yielded him greater advantages than he had won from defeat.

Farinmail, whose wrath was soon appeased, was the chief obstacle to this comfortable settlement of the new lands. He had now five hundred horsemen, and each of these was accustomed to carry an archer behind him on short expeditions. Stragglers, those employed in marking out the allotments of land, provision convoys, and even considerable bodies of troops in warlike array suffered at the hands of the men of Gwent. Loose formations could not stand before a charge of cavalry, while the solid wedge offered an easy mark to the arrow. Well-mounted parties on the hill tops signalled with their lances to those below, warning them of every movement.

Vortipore all this time took no part, exercised no influence in public affairs; he was utterly prostrated by the shocks, physical and moral, he had undergone during the last few days. The sudden uprising of crimes dead, buried, and forgotten years ago, and with the crimes the resurrection of victims, accusers, and witnesses,—all this, followed by a concussion of the brain, exasperated by an untimely drinking bout, left him with nerves disordered and unstrung. He lay silent or querulous; insensible, or at least indifferent, to external impressions; then morbidly irritable and scared at every sight and sound.

His condition paralysed his party, the chiefs of which, like the rest of the world, were excluded from his presence, and could not pretend to act or speak in his name. The power devolved upon the Praefect of the city who was second in authority, and who in the emergency secured the obedience, more or less hearty, of all. Even Bronwen, his darling, was seldom allowed to visit him, and was received with shuddering affection.

She was more lonely than ever since the evasion of her Saxon playmate.

Iorwerth shut himself up with his vile parasites and miserable slaves, and recompensed himself for past suffering by continuous debauch. His luxury was as sordid and spiritless as his other modes of selfishness, and reproduced the vices without the magnificence of Nero.

On the evening after the retreat of the fleet (no one ventured to tell him of its advance) unwonted and unwelcome company took part in his pleasures. Rhys and Smith, in the course of their systematic examination of the palace, came to a wooden structure, from the inside of which issued sounds of flute and tabor. It was provided with wooden shutters, so disposed as to admit air and light to a room below while they excluded the rain. They soon found a position in which, by turning two or three bars, they could see what passed beneath them without being exposed to observation.

As their eyes became accustomed to the

glare of light they beheld a large and
lofty hall, at one end of which was a platform raised about three feet from the floor.
Above this a rope was tightly strained and
hung about with garlands. Fauns and
nymphs capered on the rope, imitating in
rhythmical movements the gathering of the
vintage and the pressing of the grapes.
Antic monsters came and went, and at last
Silenus ascended, his huge paunch unfit for
feats of activity. Resting his hand on the
shoulder of a Bacchante, he held out a goblet
to be filled by another. His reeling steps and
frequent slips, which seemed to promise no
counterfeit catastrophe, afforded gross delight
to the spectators, some of whom testified
their admiration by laughter and applause
as the scene-ended.

Rhys and Smith tried to obtain a view of
the party for whose enjoyment the spectacle
was prepared, and distinguished three couches
arranged on three sides of a square with
three figures in scanty attire on each couch.
Nothing was visible of those reclining on

the middle bed but the tops of their heads
and their backs, as they lay immediately
beneath the shutter where Rhys and Smith
had posted themselves; moreover, the light
was concentrated on the stage, and the other
parts of the hall remained in comparative
gloom, white figures glancing to and fro,
ministering to the host and his guests.

Soon a rippling stream of music recalled
attention to the stage. Singers lined the
back of the platform, while the pantomimes
disposed themselves in picturesque groups
in front. The former described the cool
twilight, the saffron rays of Phœbus dispelling
the cloud of night, the quire of waking birds,
the spotted deer bending long necks to crop
the fragrant, dewy herbage.

The Lady of the silver bow, in succinct
vest, taller by the head and neck than her
companions, leads forth the virgin train who,
with modulated steps and graceful gesture,
express the action of the chace. The harps
are touched with firmer and more rapid quill,
the movement of the dancers grows excited

and eager, horns sound, arrows fly; while voices chant the swift flight of the deer, and his death-wound inflicted by the shaft of the goddess.

Again the music varies, changing to graver tones and a more languid measure. In verse of happier time the chorus shows the earth fainting and still beneath the burning Sun-god, who hangs midway between rising and setting. It counsels Titania, avoiding the meridian heat, to retire to the vale of Gar-gaphie till the shadows lengthen. There, hidden in deep shade of pine-woods and the pointed cypress, wells the sacred fountain in cool caves, where nature seems to simulate designs of art.

Thither, weary with the chace, the huntress wanders, thirsting for the cold, the lucid stream which bubbles under arches moulded by time in living rock. To the nymphs she delivers the unerring weapons: javelin, quiver, and loosened bow; one receives on her arms the ingrained palla, others unlace the jewelled buskins; Rhanis and Nephele, with Hyale

and Psecas, fill with water capacious urns;
while river-born Crocale twines with defter
fingers the scattered profusion of golden hair.

With swaying cadence of body and limb
the girls translate into action the choral song.
Hapless Actæon is about to appear.

Smith's saucer eyes were devouring the
wondrous show, admiring and marvelling
what it all might mean, when a sudden movement attracted them to his friend. Rhys had
found an opening from which he could espy
the occupants of the principal couch, and
now with outstretched arm was poising a
heavy knife between his finger and thumb.
It fell like a streak of light close to the head
of one of the figures below, so close as to
cut the wreath of roses on her brow, and
stuck quivering in the wood.

A shrill, ear-splitting scream rang out,
followed by another and yet another, as
Smith promptly drew Rhys back, and closing
the opening led him away.

They ran along the terraces and dropped
into the street. When they were at a safe

distance from the palace, Smith remonstrated—

"What fiend urged you to such a deed. That is not the way to revenge but to detection. Remember the word, 'torch and sword.'"

Rhys was chuckling to himself, and made no answer.

"Are you mad?" asked the other. "Have you forgotten the watchword?"

"'Torch and sword,' a good word, but that is the last word."

"Last word!" said Smith. "I should think it is the last word. When you have burnt a man's house and cut his throat, you ought to be satisfied. What more can you want after that?"

"Nothing after, oh, nothing after," replied Rhys, with deprecating gesture, "but much before. There are fine feelings, delicate susceptibilities. Saints and fathers, how she screamed!" And Rhys laughed.

"I don't understand all this," said Smith sullenly.

" I will enlighten you ; " and Rhys laid his hand on his friend's shoulder. " You were explaining yesterday how you sometimes satisfy your vindictive feelings by making a spread eagle of your enemy, or eviscerating him by walking him round and round a stake, with details too numerous to recapitulate. These are barbarous modes of torture—perfectly rudimentary."

" Use shorter words, if I am to learn your meaning," growled Smith.

" Well then," said Rhys, still laughing ; " you thought, of course, that I meant to kill her when I dropped the knife."

" Of course you meant to kill her, else why do it ? "

" You heard her scream ? "

" Heard her scream ! I think I hear her now. Ugh !"

" Perhaps you do, we are not out of range here," said Rhys blandly, "and she is capable of going on like that for an hour together. When you think she is exhausted, she will break out again as lively as ever. If she see a mouse or a spider—if any one find fault, your ears ring. I used to dislike it."

" I dare say you did," Smith answered, " but with a ground-ash stick and a little good will, the fault might be amended."

" I would not have it amended, dear friend; I would not have it amended ; it is the engine wherewith I shall work. Listen! Even you, with your heathen indifference to wounds and death, how would you like sharp knives falling into your season of convivial relaxation ; your careless ease disturbed by inexplicable sounds and warnings—casual arrows quivering in your nuptial bedpost. It would derange even your equanimity."

Smith shook his ears in modified assent.

" What then will be the condition of this woman after a few such agreeable surprises as I have in store for her. Constrain your imagination and describe her state."

" Well," said Smith, scratching his head to stimulate the faculty invoked ; " it seems to me that she will be like one of those great bows on the wall yonder. Touch a peg, and she will let fly a yell fit to split an oak plank a hand-breadth thick. I have seen them do it, meaning the bow; a shield is no good against it."

"You put it very well. Now the man is a pampered coward, as cruel as he is self-indulgent. Sometimes, instead of pretty scenes such as you saw to-night, he amuses himself by torturing those who have offended or annoyed him, or even those against whom he has no grudge, from mere wantonness. I have made inquiries about his ways, and have given wine to loose the tongues of his slaves. Some are suspended by the thumbs or other parts, and beaten with rods or scourges; some have boiling oil poured into their ears, or sharp sand cunningly introduced into their knee-joints. One of his toys is a copper kettle with shackles for the ankles. The victim is fastened to a seat, with his feet fixed in the vessel, cold water is poured in and fire put under it till the water boils. He has devices of infinite cruelty. How long will he endure this screaming love? He will tire of her suddenly—hate her. He shall punish her, and then" (Rhys was grim enough now) "then I will punish him. Torch and sword at last."

"You understand these matters better than I," said Smith, after a pause; "but our way is more straightforward."

" Direct methods will not avail here; we must wind about to our ends. The tower is too high to scale; I will get the key of the secret stair. Come in, and drink some of the old wine, and we will talk more at length and be merry."

" If I may advise," said Smith, " you will take the wine to the guard-chamber by the postern, and give your friends there a carouse; then, if questions are asked, they will readily swear that we have been there ever since darkness set in, and they will believe what they swear, which is the perfection of false witness."

" My wise friend!" exclaimed Rhys; "and I called you a barbarian!" then disappearing within his house he left Smith at the door.

He presently returned with a wine-jar, which he handled delicately, and the two men went together to the guard-chamber.

The plastered walls of this dingy cell were scrawled with rude designs done in charcoal, or scratched with a rusty nail; they were inscribed with rough verses, in which it was hard to sift the praise from the satire, while sentiments of affection disguised themselves in unexpected and ambiguous phrase.

When the friends came to the doorway—for there was no actual door—Tudur was sketching with the burnt end of a stick an historical study, wherein Julius was depicted with prodigious nose and laurelled brow, but otherwise like Polyphemus, flinging pebbles at the Saxon fleet which fled from his fury. Several vessels were sinking; and on the poop of the largest was the guileful Ulysses, whose teeth were broken by one of the stones.

"Welcome, stout Rhys!" shouted the artist, "and welcome, Smith, and a double welcome to the third guest! By my faith, this is no

native crudity in autochthonic pig-skin, but
a dainty jar from over the sea, lined with
scented pitch, filled with the mellow juice of
a more genial clime, and bearing the seal
of an artist. Bring, oh boy, cool water and
the festive horn !"

A slave brought water cold from the well,
and the apparatus for drinking. Tudur
mingled equal quantities of water and wine
in a beechen bowl, and using a dipper with
recurved handle, filled the horn with the
mixture. This drinking vessel, a curved
bull's-horn, with rim, cover, chain, and stand
of silver elaborately chased, was guard-room
property, the legacy of an ancient boon companion of the city guard. It was preserved
at the house of Meredith, one of the guard,
who dwelt hard by, and who was sworn with
awful and mysterious forms to keep the
precious relic as his life. Not to lose sight
of it, he attended any solemnity at which the
vessel was required, and was bound by virtue
of his oath not to be drunk. Tudur and
Grynn the son of Penpigon, with Meredith

and the other two, sat on heavy benches at a battered table, and a smoky, two-beaked lamp, swinging from the grimy vault, shed an uncertain light on the festivity.

Tudur drank, not by putting the horn to his lips, but holding it aloof and removing a peg at the small end, he allowed a slender, curving stream to spout into his mouth without spilling a drop. He pronounced that the wine came from the banks of Rhodanus, probably the produce of vineyards near Vienna, and he was an authority in such matters. Had he not, as he often said, traded to Gades and sojourned in Massilia, where he was supposed to have acquired a tincture of Greek refinement and taste from descendants of the Phocaean colonists?

Tudur tried to persuade the others to drink in his foreign fashion.

" For the sake of neatness and cleanliness, there being but one horn."

" Ay, ay," sighed Grynn, after a deep draught, " we know your tricks, master traveller. This is too good to be wasted in choking the simple-minded. We drink like sober men who feel the importance of what they are doing; and speaking of important matters reminds me, neighbour Rhys, that I desire your help and countenance in removing those heaps of ruin which cumber the backs of our houses. Rats swarm there, dogs come to hunt the rats, children come to pelt the dogs, mothers come and spank the children, and the barking, the shouting, the scolding, the squalling, are unspeakable."

"Then do not speak of it," Meredith put in.

" Nose and eyes are in no better case than ears. Every one casts dirt and offal there, and the smells! Then as to the sights——"

" In the name of the martyrs clap a spigot in his mouth. Pass the horn! and Tudur, a song with sea-breeze and sunshine in it to take away the taste of all that nastiness."

" Tudur hummed a stave or two, shook his head, and said—

" There is a song the crews of wine ships sing as they coast along the Mediterranean

in fine weather; but it suits a summer sea
better than a smoky guard-room, and needs
some changes."

Then with clear voice he sang—

> Our vineyards lie where merry Gaul
>   Basks in the summer air;
> Far comes the wine to cheer us all,
>   So far we banish care.
> *Chorus*—With oars that row, and winds that blow—
>   Afar we banish care.

> With gentle hand the jar incline,
>   And stoop by just degrees—
> The joys of life are in the wine,
>   Its cares are in the lees.
> *Chorus*—With oars that row, and winds that blow—
>   Our cares are in the lees.

> The lamplight in the nectar shines
>   To point where pleasures are,
> Within the rim, whose orb enshrines
>   Our purple evening star.
> *Chorus*—With oars that row, and winds that blow
>   Toward the evening star.

> False though the cup as Circe's eyes,
>   Guileful as Proteus' home,
> Bright visions with the bubbles rise,
>   As Venus from the foam.

The last chorus was interrupted by Laelius going the rounds.

" How now ? " he said, " What a riotous watch is this ! Ah, I guessed the horn was here. You have not seen any suspicious characters about—how should you ? There has been a disturbance at the palace, an attempt to assassinate Prince Iorwerth. To escape further relaxation of discipline, we will see the bottom of that jar before we go. Fill the horn, but mix not; I have no time to drink water. Wine of the Rhodanus as I live; no wonder you were chirping. I drank it in my youth. In memory of that innocent time, another horn. One more to prevent Meredith breaking his oath. And now masters get you gone ; and you Tudur and Grynn keep a better watch."

CHAPTER VI.

NAVIGATORS tell us that in the far Erythraean waters, whence come the finest and most costly pearls, the warm, sparkling surface has a current distinct from the daily tides. In the wide, prosperous deep it may pass unheeded by the careless, but in straits and perilous passages it is visible and audible as it foams and roars against any obstruction. The diver, who plunges deeply to win the treasures of ocean, knows that far down beside the rock's broad base in an opposite direction a colder current flows.

So those who penetrate beneath the social surface find forces countervailing the wavering stratum, in which float vessels of shallow burden. So he who searches deeply into his

motives for belief or action may find op-
posing currents and strange eddies, happy
if when rising gasping to the air he holds in
his basket the pearls of modesty and wisdom.

Especially in days of oppression and persecution do the under currents run fiercely.
Conspiracies to cut off the chief agent of un-
righteousness, secret societies to rectify all
that is amiss, are plentiful as weeds in the
sluggard's garden.

Renatus was the head of a secret organization for promoting the interests of the
orthodox party in Anderida. During a long
period the Pelagians had the upper hand in
Britain, and the missions of Germanus and
Lupus exercised only a transient influence.
The orthodox enjoyed great liberty of
cursing, as Gildas shows; and there is no
reason to suppose that they were persecuted
except in being restrained from persecuting
others, which is doubtless a hardship to men
penetrated with a sense of duty. If we are
sure that we are the sole depositaries of truth
necessary to salvation, we are right in using

all means, even persecution, to bring men to the obedience of that truth. Does not Providence persecute those who are false, idle, cowardly, and dirty.

At the time when Renatus returned from Gaul his friends were in a state of unusual depression. The reaction in favour of native ways was in full swing. Kent, usually most susceptible to influence from beyond the sea, was conquered by the heathen Jutes. The miserable remnant that escaped slaughter were slaves, and if Christian worship did not wholly cease, yet the cry of the broken and desolate to their Father in heaven is too urgent to concern itself about niceties of doctrine.

In inverse proportion to their low estate were the zeal and bitterness of the orthodox. Tepid adherents had gone with the popular stream, those who remained were free from scruple, indifference, and misgiving. They considered patriotism a narrow and somewhat dangerous sentiment, whose pretensions should never be allowed to compete with the claims of religion. Little they recked of the triumph of heathen strangers if their own heretical countrymen were punished. Few lived to expiate their crime, and to forget in the anguish of thraldom the jealous quarrel with their brethren.

Renatus certainly did not go all lengths with these zealots, but where the line of division was drawn he did not know. He had always been connected with their party, and to all appearance shared their views, but his aims were higher. He gave his ability and eloquence, and used the organization of the society to carry out more easily certain ends of his own. He did not ask himself where and why he differed from his allies nor how far personal wrongs influenced his conduct. There were depths into which he dared not pry, for somewhere down in those obscure caverns was a naked, furious something; the ruin of what was once a reasonable man; the wreck, it might be, of himself.

In the horror of this vision he longed for help and sympathy from a strong man, a man like Julius—one to whom such terrors were idle dreams; one firm, collected, clear as adamant. The Praefect seemed to be the complement of his own organization, endowed with just the qualities wherein he felt himself deficient. If Julius could be won to the true faith, and why should he not? what service might be expected from his knowledge of men, his insight and foresight, his fearless readiness for every contingency. What a pillar of support would such a character be to his own moral edifice, what an auxiliary in the great enterprise now at hand, the thought of which was the only spell to conjure the hideous goblin that lurked in his heart.

It was not a case of converting a heretic stubbornly wedded to his depraved doctrines. This man was simply indifferent; one whose devotion was paid to all that is great and noble—a student of Epictetus, an admirer of Antoninus, a mild censurer of the super-stition and dirty habits of Julian. Surely to such a temper it would not be difficult to present, in attractive guise, the highest and purest development of religion. Surely Christianity, if it had a fair hearing, would be preferred to the harsh and hazy system whose last word to suffering humanity is, " If you can no longer endure your lot, the door is open—depart !" It were blasphemy to suppose that the religion of benevolence and beneficence, which inculcates, next to the love of God, love to our brother and our neighbour, should yield to the doctrine that wife and children and friends should be subjects of indifference to the wise and good man, because at all times he is liable to lose them. This was, perhaps, not quite a fair way of putting the matter, but Renatus was not deeply read in the Stoical philosophy.

Julius, on his side, had been struck with the boldness and eloquence of Renatus, and was disposed to let the bishop settle matters with the " fellow from Gaul " as best he might. Subsequent inquiries brought out fragments of a tale of wrong sustained by Renatus with dignity and courage, and also the circumstance that he was a Roman by paternal descent. The Praefect thought it a pity that the powers of such a man should be wasted in theological squabbles, and had found an opening for the employment of his abilities.

So it fell out that each had a place in the other's thoughts, and opportunity alone was lacking for an interchange of ideas, when on mounting the steps of the seaward rampart on the morning after the repulse of the fleet, Renatus found himself within a few yards of the Praefect.

Julius stood on a temporary platform which projected from the parapet, superintending the arrangement of some stakes in the mud below. Already a double row of oaken piles, with the pointed ends towards the sea, had been set firmly in the clay, and a third row was being planted quincunx fashion.

Renatus determined to take the offered chance, but not wishing to be intrusive, he leaned over the battlement and said, as if to himself—

"To what end are these preparations for defence ? "

"This is the only spot," said Julius, not looking directly at the speaker, "the only place of any extent, where ships can approach so near the wall as to lay ladders from their decks."

"Do you not know,". Renatus said, looking earnestly at the other, "that there is a better defence for cities than walls, however thick and high ; than engines, however powerful."

"Truly," Julius answered, "the virtue of her citizens was Sparta's rampart, but this is no Sparta. We are not equal to the Saxons in natural strength, therefore we avail ourselves of artificial defences, and where the lion's hide will not stretch we eke it out with the skin of the fox. We find it easier to regulate our tormenta," and he pointed to the catapults on the adjacent tower, "than our pleasures, and a bulwark of stone is a tolerable substitute for fortitude if we are not called on to bear it about with us."

"Temperance and fortitude are no mean virtues, but more is required of man, and man requires more. Sparta was an anachronism of savage polity, a recoil from barbarous softness. Founded on the sword, where is she now? Where all that is so built must be."

"Where we shall be before many days are past, if you are a prophet."

"Let the event show what I am. It shall be more tolerable for Sodom and Gomorrah than for this city. But to you I have a special message. Lot, who was not of the accursed seed, was not doomed to perish in the overthrow of the sinners."

"And pray," said Julius blandly, the conversation not taking the turn he desired, "which of the cardinal virtues is that history designed to illustrate?"

"Justice and mercy," answered Renatus. "Those were hours of darkness, or at most of the earliest dawn. Do you, who sneer, do you, standing in clear daylight, act as becomes your better knowledge?"

"Yes. The work which comes to me I perform to the best of my power; perfect or imperfect, what can man do more?"

"More!" cried Renatus, "do you ask what more? He can seek for higher and nobler work, and, if his present task be well done, a loftier sphere of toil will be allotted to him. Shall we count him happy who attains to his own ideal? How low must that ideal be! The blind mole burrowing in the earth fulfils her purpose and is content, the bird which seeks the sky does not reach her goal."

"Your high-flying bird is not usually the best nest-builder," Julius retorted. Then to those below—"Keep that stake at the same slope as the others, and the notch for the cross-beam at the right level." He turned again to Renatus with the question—"Can any duty which God enjoins be considered low? But if no duty be low, none can be high. We are not free from interruption here. If you are at leisure to visit my house a little after sunset, I will gladly snatch an hour from sleep to converse with you on a more practical topic."

Renatus willingly assented, and bent his way to the Basilica, wondering what the practical topic might be.

" Nothing but a warning not to meddle with the authorities here, probably," he said to himself, " and I can easily turn that sort of talk into what channel I will.   It is well that he is disposed to argue, it will be hard if I am not more than a match for him, but I must be careful not to provoke him to anger. He who would conquer must be strong, he who would win must be gentle, he who would persuade must avoid offence."

The twilight was fading when he reached the vestibule of the Praefect's house, the evening star was just visible in the faint delicate green of the western sky, and people in the square were blocks of darkness with no details of personality.   He checked his mind, which was wandering away in a wilderness of imagery, and turning his back on the scene, beat on the door with the bronze ring which served as a knocker. The janitor opened, and a slave with a torch conducted the visitor through lounging groups of men, some armed, some equipped as runners, through the peristyle and the outer room to the study beyond.

Julius rose to receive his guest, and a slave handed him bread, fruits, and wine. Renatus took a morsel of bread that he might not appear to reject the offer of hospitality, and the slave disappeared.

The lights were so disposed as to illumine the face of Renatus, while that of the host remained in obscurity, a move which the former met by drawing the cowl over his face. Julius was the first to speak.

" You are aware, of course, that some days ago hot search was made after you, a search for which I am responsible. It was a duty which I discharged without any feeling of enmity against you, with no regret when the pursuit failed. In the course of necessary inquiries certain incidents have come to my knowledge ; secrets wonderfully kept con-

sidering the notoriety of some of the facts,
and the number of persons to whom they
must have been more or less known, and
these I have pieced together as well as I
could. The result has been that my interest
and sympathy have been awakened, and so
far from wishing to add to your undeserved
sufferings, I would rather help you to banish
the recollection of them by giving your mind
an occupation which will thrust out painful
thoughts. I am no stranger to your ability,
and have heard your persuasive eloquence.
Why should a man of your power drift in
vagabond purposelessness from land to land,
wasting his strength in wordy battles about
insoluble questions with such antagonists as
the Bishop of Anderida! I can imagine that
you nurse some project of vindictive justice,
of which it is not necessary nor would it be
becoming in me to speak. It is enough that
what I have now to mention would not in
any way affect such a scheme either as helping
or hindering it."

"I have no scheme of vengeance," said

Renatus in solemn tones. " I leave the sinner to the justice of Heaven."

" Just so," said Julius ; "that is one way of putting it; but I believe it comes to much the same thing in practice. However, I will know nothing of the matter. I speak of things remote from such questions—of a career of honour, independence and useful- ness. Any proposal of employment here it were as insulting in me to offer as it would be base in you to entertain ; but if there be a post of dignity and influence in which, without sacrifice of spiritual functions, you may promote a great cause—a cause in which we shall be fellow-workers without your being under my authority, or the autho- rity of those who control me, the Pendragon alone excepted—would you esteem such an office worth your acceptance ? Would you consent to be chief minister of an indepen- dent state, bound in league with all the states of the south to make head against the heathen who are swarming to these shores in ever-increasing numbers ? The task would doubtless be heavy, and the discipline to be enforced of difficult application to these Britons, but of inestimable moral value to them; and he who bore a leading part in their deliverance would gain a position from which to exercise a mighty influence on the regenerate nation. This position is now open for your acceptance—will you despise the offer?"

Renatus answered without a moment's hesitation—

" I can despise nothing that is offered with goodwill. Kindness has not been shown to me so often as to make me undervalue it. For this offer, and for your good opinion, I thank you sincerely. My life may doubtless appear to others a purposeless drifting; it is not so really—there is a clue to the maze. That I may not appear ungrateful, I will speak of things, of purposes, which are often in my thoughts, seldom on my tongue. One subject of my care removed, my life is then devoted to one over-mastering object."

"And that object, you tell me, is not vengeance."

"It is not. I never seek him. He is thrust upon me by a higher power."

"Surely," said Julius, "the occasion was of your seeking when you pronounced doom upon us all a few days ago?" And he thought—this fellow is but a crazy fool. He can never be trusted. Then, speaking aloud, he continued, "You desire then the repentance and amendment of your enemy; you hope to meet him as a brother hereafter."

"Spare me," said Renatus, thrusting back his cowl and showing a pale face, on which drops of sweat stood thickly. "I will not deny that thoughts of revenge arise in my sinful heart; but they are not allowed, they are thrust down—down into an abyss where I fear to look. I would not be misjudged by you; rather once more open the wound, which never can be healed. A charcoal-burner saved my life. He drew me from the pool, he tended me in his hut till I was whole of my hurts. I sought to recover the fallen woman from him—from the lascivious ape

whom, for their sins, God set over this people.
The attempt was successful. It was supposed that she had committed suicide, and he
believed it gladly. I carried her over the
sea, a wreck in body and mind, and nursed
her faithfully till she somewhat recovered.
She was placed in a society of pious women,
where her soul was touched with true contri-
tion. She spent years, long years of prayer
and penance in performing menial services
for the lazars of the city where she dwelt.
You do not know what such services mean—
the horrors from which she never flinched.
I bore the wounds of my soul from shrine
to shrine, and learned that though celestial
balms may ease their aching, the only healer
is—death.

" At length, in the recent troubles, the city
was sacked, and all the sisterhood massacred
save one, whom the Franks found giving
drink to one of their own wounded comrades.
They yielded her to me, these wild men,
unhurt, and without ransom—may God
reward them ! We returned a few weeks

ago to our old refuge in the woods, there to await her release from this vile body—an enfranchisement which now cannot be afar off. One wish she has—a wish she would conceal from me, but I have discovered the secret—the longing of a mother to see her daughter—her only child—hers, not mine. To gratify her desire, that she may depart hence in peace, without a thought which may come between her soul and heaven, is my present care. Tell me, Roman, is this revenge ?"

Julius poured out wine, and, without speaking, held it towards his companion, who shook his head, but ate eagerly of the fruit, whose acid cooled his parched mouth. Presently he pushed away the dish and went on—

" That accomplished, I devote to the service of God the remainder of this shattered life. In my driftings to and fro I have learnt to speak to many a tribe in its proper tongue. To one of these tribes, Frank or Frisian, Saxon or Aleman, as opportunity shall guide,

will I carry the good news of a Redeemer ;
striving by word and work to raise their
rude hearts to religion and civility—to help
them up the first steps of the ladder which
reaches from earth to heaven, whereon divine
messengers are for ever ascending and descending.   If at the end the martyr's prize
await me, the palm of the victorious witness
for truth and holiness, that is the height of
my ambition."

"Ambition," echoed Julius, "say not ambition, that implies an object worthy of our
efforts and sacrifices.   To waste your intellect in expounding to the heavy barbarians
of black Hercynian forest or Frisian
swamp the differences between Arianism and
orthodoxy, and the true method for com-
puting the Paschal moon; and finally to have
your brains beaten out by an exasperated
neophyte in despair of apprehending these
subtleties, this we call, not ambition, but
fanaticism."

"What cause," answered Renatus, "ever
leavened the world that had not it in a strong

element of what you call fanaticism—the fire, the lightning of the heart, which rends the rocks asunder, and knows no impossibility. There are other subjects, besides those you name, concerning which we speak, whether to heathens or to nominal Christians. And as to barbarism, what were our forefathers? What but half-naked robbers, somewhat fiercer and more cunning than their neighbours."

"This is too much," exclaimed Julius, rising. "Who are you that you dare to revile and despise the fathers of the mightiest race the world has seen?"

"I do not despise them, but I maintain that their beginnings were as low and rude as those of the tribes I have named. It was a mighty race whose mission has been to reduce the world under one government, with one head, whose rule extended from Britain to India, and from the Elbe to the fountains of the Nile. When this was accomplished, decay set in, the promised Deliverer appeared, and out of the carcase of the lion came the honey of true religion. But what Christianity did for the corrupt enslaved nations of the empire is no measure of its effect on a fresh and vigorous people, whose dawn presages what their noon will be. You illustrate your walls with effigies of wonder-working men," and Renatus pointed to the stencilled portraits. " I foretell that the lustre of their exploits and marvels will pale beside the achievements of the despised savage of the Hercynian forest or the Frisian swamp. These grim giants, who to-morrow will be swarming over your walls, are not men who will weep for new worlds to conquer, rather will they seek for them, perhaps find them—who knows—discover the lost Atlantis. He who shall baptize Sicambrian Clovis will do more for the world than if he had sung like Virgil or conquered like Caesar."

" A gentle convert and an obedient your Sicambrian will be." .

" Pshaw !" said Renatus, " do you make the sword-blade and the ploughshare of wax or of iron. There is rough work to be done, and there are rough men to do it. Clear eyes and able hands will be needed to wield the sword and guide the plough for a thousand years to come. Ambition! Were I moved by mere ambition, what a career is open to him whose skill and courage shall sway the counsels of the renovated empire. Far, far beyond such petty aims my hopes aspire. I look to a grander future, when each shall love his brother for the love of Christ, when the will of God shall be the will of his free and happy creatures. The visions of the seer, the inspired songs of the prophet, shall yet be fulfilled in that glorious time when war and slavery shall be no more ; when lust of blood and greed of gain shall yield to peace and charity ; when the sick and the hungry shall be relieved in His name who satisfies us with good things and renews our youth as the eagle's. I shall not live to see that day, for there is much to do. Ages may elapse before its arrival, but come it will, and the feeblest worker may hasten its advent.

Can you, who love and seek all that is pure and beautiful, everything unselfish and noble, —can you hold back from such an enterprise? Do you see in its wide scope no room for the grandest energies? Does no inward voice cry, ' In this work my hand shall be seen, in these fields I will be no sluggard !' Lord Praefect, you said that we might be fellow-workers—we may be so. I would give my right hand to have you at my side in this conflict with the powers of darkness. What binds you here to this paltry city and its vile chief? You are not of the blood of these men ; to their Count you owe neither duty nor thanks ; in the exchange of benefits he is deeply your debtor, and pays such obligations in his accustomed coin. Give your allegiance where it is justly due—to God, and to your own true country—Rome ; she claims your services and knows their value. Fear not a cold reception, or an insufficient sphere of operations. All doors are open ; Remigius will hail you as an ally, and forward your views with all his influence. You have neither wife nor child, no tie but your possessions—too feeble a chain to hold you back. Love of power, desire of fame, I do not set before you ; they are unworthy to be named in such a cause ; but they will be gratified—power the most beneficent, ruling in the hearts of men ; fame, immortal as their spirits, will present themselves unsought. These are not our rewards. To restore the defaced image of the Creator ; to fill men's souls with the love of Christ till their lives conform ever more and more to His life these are our prizes ; and at last, whether age or sickness, or sword or fire destroy our bodies, to enjoy the approval of conscience, till our failing senses hear the harps of heaven and behold the glory that is ineffable.

"Julius Romanus, can you turn from this prospect, reject the pearls, and choose the husks of the swine-trough—prefer the service of a debased and doomed family to the call of Rome your mother, and of God. Opportunity comes but once. Do not—do not neglect it."

"If I were twenty years younger," said Julius, with unwonted hesitation; "but it is absurd ; my work is here."

"Your work lies where your special gifts are needed. Here you are pouring water into sieves ; there you are a messenger of grace." .

"No," Julius answered with a smile, "I am not the wood from which such Mercuries are carved. I lack the faith, the enthusiasm, the apostolic essence. For a moment you moved me, I confess. We must go our several ways, but count me among your friends. In that matter of your first care I can serve you and I will, and so—farewell."

As Renatus went through the dark streets the horror in his heart whispered to him. His schemes, it told him, were futile, his labours vain, and his hope a delusion. God was his enemy—the fiend his master. He spent the night in tears and broken lamentations.

CHAPTER VII.

NUMBERLESS rivers run through chasms and fissures of the mountains to subterranean seas and never emerge to the light of day. Wherever the earth is pierced we find her blood distilling from pores, streaming from crevices of the rock. In the vast deep domes of Illyrian caverns eyeless fish seek their food in night-dark lakes and rivers dull as Acheron. So man's sentient and intelligent nature, which is co-extensive with all he sees, knows, thinks, and feels, is permeated by myriad influences, dropping, uniting, interlacing, flowing ; some issuing in springs or swamps, some in latent pools, tenanted by blind groping abortions of thought and mystery, unrecognizable by even himself.

The words of Renatus, like the smoky torches of the cave, had shed an uncertain light in the mind of Julius—a flickering gleam which illuminated a narrow circle, and made the surrounding space more gloomy and disquieting. Was the task to which he had devoted his life the noblest within reach? —was it noble in any degree? Was it good at all to strive for the maintenance of such a state of things as existed in Anderida. The cause was vitiated by the faults and crimes to be upheld, and it needed no inspired prophet to announce that the catastrophe was at hand, that swift destruction was impending. To what end was he sacrificing his life and his powers of work; was the object desirable even if its attainment were feasible? He knew the doors that were open to him in Gaul, and that among Franks, Burgundians, or Visigoths, he would find friends and welcome. But to desert a cause he had once espoused —which might with his support still stand awhile—he could not do it.

With these thoughts seething in his mind

he went out into the night, followed at a
short distance by two armed attendants. He
mounted the steps by which Renatus had
ascended in the morning, and leaning against
the battlement of a tower, looked toward the
Saxon fleet and camp. Stars twinkled in the
cavernous sky and on the dun water; while
redder and more lurid lights glowed and
were reflected from the rafts where sailors
were busy raising the sunken vessels. The
harsh scream and dull shock of one of the
engines disturbed the night, as the plunging
missile broke the quivering reflections.

The young moon was gone, for it was past
midnight. The tide was high, and over the
smooth sea came voices which seemed
muffled by the soft obscurity; words which
he ought to understand but which conveyed
no meaning. The gentle puffs of air, the
lapping of little waves, the placid repose of
the hour prevailed; and relaxing the discipline
of his mind he suffered thoughts, memories,
impressions, to enter and mingle without
control. Beasts of the field, bright birds

and whatsoever dwells in the broad shining waters, were composed to sleep beneath the silent sky, and cares were soothed, and weary hearts forgot their toil. Night, the mother of sleep and of death—the rest from labour for ever—reigned, with crown of drowsy weed and dittany. No more struggles with change-able men and inflexible fates, but repose and absorption into the universal soul. Had the dreams of his youth, when there was no pleasure but in action, come to this—to a longing for dissolution in the dreary void of impersonality? Renatus had something better than this; at least he proposed to himself something higher.

But this listless questioning was useless, worse than useless, it was enervating. There was work to be done, and rousing himself with a slight shivering he returned home, and proceeding to his study, he trimmed the lamp and began to read.

It is not always easy to resume the reins after dropping them. The Praefect's mind wandered from the scroll, his spirit from the narrow room, and his head sank back on the cushions of the couch.

Through the filmy veils of slumber filtered half-heard music, and his ears were strained to listen, for he knew the enchanting sound, the song of the Sirens. Sweet as children's laughter, clear as distant trumpets, sad as a murmuring wave of the shoreless sea. The words and music are unchanged from ages to ages, the meanings are diverse as the souls of men. He had heard the descant in his eager prime, and seen the bright delusive vision, the images of beauty, of power, and of wisdom. Now he gazed on shattered, half-buried wrecks; on mute, sightless heads peering ghastly from the fruitless, time-heaped sands — heard the hollow wind sighing in deaf ears, and through thin, storm-bleached hair, while grain by grain drifting dust hid the past.

" This," he cried, " is not the Siren's shore, nor here the palace of Parthenope ! "

Immediately he stood under a wide and lofty portico, in a region strange yet familiar.

His feet had never trodden those hills, but he recognized every feature, and could name each point and island ; from the Surrentine vineyards and the promontory of Minerva, by the mouldering splendours of Capreae, by Inarime the shuddering tomb of Typhon, by Prochyta to ancient Cumae.

The blue sea, crisped by passing breezes to hues of violet, shone between tall, fluted shafts of African marble, whose rich, creamy yellow tints were enhanced by the crimson bloom of roses. The white marble pavement was studded with stars of bloodstone, gold-veined jasper, and lapis lazuli, and surrounded by a deep border of intertwining mosaic scrolls. The wall at the back was painted in panels divided from each other by pilasters of green marble with gilt flutings, and in front of the panels were bronze statues of the twelve Caesars on serpentine pedestals. A colossal chryselephantine figure of Rome with spear and helmet occupied the central space.

Couches of rare and beautiful woods, inlaid with ivory and tortoiseshell, were covered

with woven and embroidered tapestries from
the east, and over a table was thrown a
feather-cloth, whose ground was of peacock
eyes, and the pattern wrought with plumage
of the swan, the kingfisher, and the flamingo.

On the marble terrace in front of the
portico a tall fountain tossed its wavering
spray, which fell again, now with cool patter-
ing on the shining brim, now with deeper
bubbling sound in the water of the basin.
Broad white steps led to other terraces
fragrant with orange and lemon trees,
bordered with aloe and cactus. On one
side, the portico looked on a shady hill where
wood-pigeons cooed from the lofty chestnuts,
and the open space was studded with clumps
of myrtle, arbutus, and bay. The other end
gave a view of Baiae and the Lucrine Lake.
Like a golden sickle edged with foam the
strand curved away toward Misenum; and
over green woods and vineyards and bright
villas, the Epomean mount seemed to melt
into the soft sky.

Over the broad marbles happy, virginal

Psyche wandered, unvext of Venus, untempted by malignant sisters.

All these details were apprehended at once, as usually happens when objects are seen directly by the mind, without the intervention of the eyes.

A voice was heard without, the voice of Renatus, crying—

" Fair and lovely is the surface—but, beside you is the lake Avernus ; beneath your feet are the caverns of hell ! "

A swift wind brought a cloud across the sun, a shadow over the sea. The flowers bent their heads, the draperies in front of the dreamer waved. The chill blast struck him, and with one last glance at the fruitful earth, the fair abodes of men, the ships, like swans in the sea, and the cloud sailing under the sunny heaven, he was whirled away like a leaf in October to the street of tombs.

The light, tender, shell-less soul flew down by lines of grim mansions with doors but no windows ; no sibyl with golden bough marshalled the way, no angel of death,

beautiful, stern, yet tender. Down before the
icy breath of destiny it flew ; down by walls
of living rock behind which lay dead shells,
the serpentine exuviae of men ; down the
dark and dubious hollows which lead to the
abyss.

The soul, though destitute of bodily organs,
smelled the graveolent vapours of Avernus as
it swept onward among myriads of similar
shadows to a boundless hall, whose firmament
of wet rock gleamed here and there with the
pale, phosphorescent light of spectres. Here
they sat at a visionary banquet where none
spoke or stirred, and there was a sound of
water dropping from the roof into pools
below. Every drop was reverberated under
dim arches till the dripping echoes seemed
infinite, and with every drop a soul faded
away. For years, that might be endless, they
sat in grey, weary vacuity, and the huge
bones of the earth pressed them down.

The soul of Julius sank with deadly faint-
ness. Its hour was come to be absorbed in
the universe.

Again the voice of Renatus was heard through the ceaseless dropping—

"To him who knows the better and chooses the worse is granted the fulfilment of his desire."

But the tenacious soul rallied its wavering powers, and burst the bonds of dumbness with a cry—

"To do the duty which comes to hand—to do it rightly, strenuously—is the essence of philosophy and of religion."

Julius awoke with the cry on his lips. A sudden summer storm had passed over the city, and the rain was still dropping from the eaves. A gust of cold damp air from the open window had extinguished the lamp—the wick smouldering sent forth graveolent vapours.

The slave who brought a fresh light was amazed to find his grave, reserved master laughing like a boy.

CHAPTER VIII.

THE grey light of dawn struggled through the mist, but the eye could with difficulty make out the source of various sounds which broke the morning stillness. There were masts and dark hulls imperfectly seen, the mouth of a muddy creek, and armed men appearing and fading away in the damp atmosphere. It was a squadron sent to gather supplies for the fleet, and the scene was the rich marshes about six leagues eastward from Anderida, not far from the frontier of the Kentish Jutes, a country abounding in cattle, and hitherto unplundered.

Ælle had taken the three ships which brought the last band of adventurers from Old Saxony, giving in exchange allotments of land. These, when fitted out, were placed under the command of Eormenred of the Old House, and sent to strengthen the fleet before Anderida. They arrived the day after the repulse of the assault, and were despatched to the eastward by Cymen the same evening.

Three war galleys, and four vessels of heavier burden, lay in the mud at the mouth of the little stream which entered the sea near the point of junction between the sand-stone hills and the marshes. Each galley furnished seventy-five men fully armed, and each of the heavy craft a score of active lads provided with seax and javelin. They moved off in divisions, keeping by the side of the stream, the light-armed exploring in front and covering the right flank. Any creature, human or canine, which came in their way was promptly disposed of lest an alarm should be raised, and in this manner, concealed by the mist, they made their way two leagues into the country following the general direction of the hills. They then spread themselves in a line more than a league in length, and began marching steadily toward the sea. They surrounded every house or group of houses, and slew the in-dwellers, but spared the slaves to serve as guides and for driving the cattle. These men owed no love to their former masters, and readily showed the Saxons the points to be occupied in order to secure the largest amount of booty.

Meantime, as the day advanced, the fog lifted and the smoke raised by those who remained with the ships marked the spot to which the foragers were returning. The cattle were in large enclosures, the ditches of which were at once fences and drains, while bridges of logs squared on the upper surface gave access to the fields and roads. Hour after hour the quest continued ; an ever-increasing throng of sheep and cattle, with carts carrying grain, flour, and miscellaneous plunder poured toward the coast, where the first arrivals were already being embarked.

Eormenred, on the eastern flank of the

line, which was most exposed to attack,
watched a town which at no great distance
stood on a gentle slope rising a few feet
above the dead level of the surrounding
country. It was a haven of the sea, and
many masts could be discerned among the
houses, though the glare of the sun pre-
cluded accurate observation. It was no part
of his business now to plunder towns, and
he determined not to interfere at all with
the place, lest the citizens should be put on
the alert, and perhaps acquire a bad habit of
concealing their wealth—the wealth which
he held to be his own if he had strength
and leisure to take it. To meddle pre-
maturely would be to diminish the stock
of honey which these excellent bees were
storing up for the benefit of himself and his
friends. Accordingly, he avoided the neighbourhood of the town, and turned his
marauders in a westerly direction. Nevertheless, as chance would probably give them
at some future time occasion of entering
into possession of their own, it would be

advisable to examine the property—to recon-
noitre the approaches and defences—to spy
out any spots where the place might be most
conveniently assaulted.

Accordingly, picking out fifty of his most
active followers, and ten of the best of those
lightly armed, he approached the town, while
the rest of the men drove the spoil to the
ships.

Eormenred made a circuit toward the sea
to get a better view, and as he drew nearer
he was aware of a great noise and disturbance in that direction, and expressed an
angry hope that no one was presuming to
meddle with " our town."

He advanced under cover of a dyke, the
earth from which had been thrown up on the
inner side to form a raised road convenient
in wet seasons, and beyond this road roofs
of farm buildings appeared.   Shrieks and
angry exclamations were heard, and blows,
not as of men fighting but as of men being
killed.   He pressed on cautiously to a bridge
where the road descending allowed a view

of what was going on within, and the sight made his blood boil. A band of pirates was attacking a comfortable farm-house, surrounded by rich land, which stood in the large enclosure with orchard and garden, newly mown hay, and old stacks, fields of wheat and barley, beans and lupines, with implements of peaceful husbandry scattered about.

The rustics fought with sithe and hayfork, but such weapons in such hands were little help against men in mail, whose trade was war. The master lay dead across his threshold and the women shrieked within— the ploughman fell beside the shepherd, and the munching oxen looked with large eyes at their driver gasping in his blood. Two long-armed mowers stood in the ox-cart, and the pirates recoiled with gaping wounds from the swing of the sithes; another sweep of the rough-edged blade shore off an axe-man's left hand, but a cunning sea rover divided the leather which held the pole to the yoke, and the cart tipping up threw the sithe-men among their enemies. A fierce dog sprang from beneath it, pinned one of the assailants by the throat and brought him to the ground. The beast did not worry, but just made his teeth meet, and held on ; he was cut to pieces, but before the strong jaws could be unlocked the robber was dead.

Although these proceedings were very well in accordance with the designs of Woden, as Eormenred had expounded them to Julius at the council, they filled his soul with fury; but he put a weight on his wrath and kept it down, till he should see an advantageous way of ascertaining the wishes of the All-Father by a trial of strength.

At this moment a slave, who had profited by the confusion to lay hands on a bag of coin, came flying over the bridge, hotly pursued by several of the plunderers. Eormenred lugged out his sword and ran to the bridge, where, wasting no time in words, he fell upon the foremost of the interloping villains and with a back-handed stroke smote off his head. The rest, though surprised and some-deal

dismayed at the apparition of an enemy in
such force, kept a good countenance, and
while one stood at bay in the middle of the
bridge, wrought hard to break it down. But
the solid oaken beams could neither be cut
through nor dislodged in so short a time as
was allowed.

As Eormenred came on, the man in front
swung aloft a heavy axe with a four-foot
helve. He stood with his right foot a little
advanced, rose on tiptoe, and slid his right
hand down to his left as the blow descended.
A Roman would have killed his man with a
straight thrust, but the Saxons had blunt
points. Eormenred raised his shield on
high, met the axe before it had acquired its
full momentum and by yielding broke its
force. Nevertheless it cut through the iron
boss, cleft the cross-grained linden boards,
and reached the arm which upheld them. The
pirate tore open the shield with a dexterous
wrench, but before he could recover his
weapon, Eormenred's sword struck him be-
twixt the ear and the right shoulder, shearing

clean through the collar-bone. The blood spouted out in a bright red arch, rising in jets, and he fell as a sack of corn falls on the floor. Eormenred stepped over him, and was confronted by three who stood round the bridge end with uplifted axes. The Saxons were uncertain what to do, their leader's broken shield was rather an encumbrance than a defence, and to make a rush would drive him headlong under the axes, perhaps sacrifice him. They sounded the slimy ditch with sticks and spear-shafts, but between mud and water it was no ways fordable; moreover, it was above twelve feet in width of water, and considerably more from grass to grass, with slippery, rotten sides, and a bad take off.

While they hesitated, Eomaer, Eormen-red's son, a fine lad of seventeen, had flung off helmet, hauberk, and sword-belt; and now, just as the axes were about to fall, he took his run, and with a bound like a deer cleared the space, lighted fairly on his feet, and drove his scax to the handle between the ribs of the right hand pirate. This one, staggering from the shock, fell across his neighbour and spoiled his blow, while Eormenred cut through the helve of the third axe. The Saxons, charging over the bridge, made short work of the stragglers running to the assistance of their comrades. Seven pirates, standing in a circle, made a stout defence, but they were overwhelmed with javelins, stones, and blocks of wood, till one dropped covered with wounds; then the ring was broken and all were slain.

Some stripped the dead and laid the armour and weapons in a cart, some attended to the wounded, and some drove away the cattle and other spoil. Eormenred bid men take wisps from the burning ricks and fire the thatch to let other bands know that nothing was to be got there.

The walls of the farm-house and out-buildings were constructed with mud and reeds; but there was a ruinous tower of stone in one corner of the enclosure, the work of a more laborious race than the

present inhabitants of the marshes. Hither
Eormenred, having sent on the plunder,
came with a satisfied conscience to meditate.
Though the upper platform was barely
twenty feet above the ground, it commanded
an extensive view of the alluvial lands. He
looked back on the fields he had desolated,
and on the willow-fringed river eastward,
beyond which herds might be seen moving
to places more secure. Then he looked to
the town, which was not more than a mile
away, and counted four war ships on the
beach; and he thought he could see the
masts of others further round, but these last
might be traders.

The crews were attacking the southern
gate of the town, kindling a great fire against
it, and from the smoke on the other side it
might be presumed that the river gate was
attempted in the same manner. So far the
inhabitants seemed to hold their own as well
as it could be seen from such a distance.

Eormenred sat down on a stone to think,
and he thought slowly, holding his head in

both hands and resting his elbows on his knees.

The Ætheling had sent him to collect provisions, that must be the first point, and it was nearly accomplished. They must be sent safely, that was the second. Then information must be given of this pirate squadron, which, instead of joining Ælle, was plundering on its own account. So far all was clear.

He rose and sent a messenger to the creek, bidding the skippers push on the lading of the ships with all speed, and get the war galleys afloat as soon as the tide was high enough.

Then he called for a runner, and while the man was coming looked again toward the town. The fire was low ; but trains of men, like ants, were bringing beams, planks, rafters, and such matters, and casting them into the flame, and many were seen to fall as if shot from above, and dark bodies lay about the sands.

The runner came—a long, lean, deep-chested man, with thin, wide nostrils, lumps of muscle high up in the calf of the leg, clean tendons, and high-arched instep.

"You see yon high land," said Eormenred, "lying between south and sunset, but nearer sunset; how far is it?"

"It is over an hour with these marshes to cross and bridges few."

"Two hours thence will bring you to the Ætheling. When you come to the flat beyond the hills take a horse, if you can see a good one which can be got without loss of time. If you deliver the message under the three hours keep the horse for your pains."

The man grinned, drew his belt tight, and put a smooth pebble in his mouth.

"You shall say to the Ætheling, 'There are four, probably more, ships of a strange folk plundering on our coast, attacking a town before the eyes of me, Eormenred. The supplies of cattle and grain shall be sent with due heed; but hence go these strangers not without fighting. Be they more or less I will have to do with them, but see not yet how it were best to begin. Let the Ætheling take counsel and act as behoves.' Begone!"

The runner started not at a great pace as it appeared; but covering much ground at a stride, he was soon out of sight.

Eormenred sat down again to work out the other and more difficult part of his duty—the punishment of these wretches who were not afraid to trespass on lands intended for the support and solace of better men. The regular vikings of the fleet had openly scorned him, Eormenred, as a land-lubber, fit to drive oxen, and therefore proper for such expeditions as the present. They should see that he could handle a ship and fight a ship. They should see—Gr-r-r! Awful sounds came through his bushy, stubborn beard. But he must be wary as well as bold. The odds were at least two to one against him. The shipmen judged, from their arms and equipment, that these knaves were from the Scandinavian gulf, sturdy fighters, who seldom showed their backs to an enemy. Even if he fell suddenly on their rear, or caught them scattered for plunder and discomfited them, the remnant would get away in the ships, and he wanted these ships for a trophy to show what he had done.

It was no use; his brain was getting thick with thinking; he would take a spell of hard work to clear it. Perhaps toward evening there might be a favourable opening.

So he left his neighbour Sæbyrht and his son Eomaer to keep watch on the tower while he went to the creek, where he turned to with a will and so stimulated the rest by his example, that each man did the work of two. By six hours after noon the ships were laden and awaited the farther rising of the tide to be gone.

Just then Eomaer came in breathless, and cried—

"The pirates have got into the town, father, and it is burning in five places, and I have been close up to them, for they keep no look out, and I counted seven war ships, and the two nearest of them are almost afloat, for they came ashore later in the ebb than the

others, and we can take these two easily, for
there is cover of trees, and walls, and sand-
hills to within a furlong of them, and
Sæbyrht bid me run and tell you all
about it."

"My mates," shouted Eormenred; "you
hear what the boy says! These sea thieves
are destroying—taking away our goods.
Shall we endure this wrong, this insult—
taking them under our very noses? We are
robbed—slapped in the face, and we say,
'Thank you kindly.' Shall we go back and
be laughed at—pointed at?"

"No!" roared the men. "Settle what is
to be done and we will do it. Let us get at
them, that's all."

There was a hurried council in which it
was decided that Eormenred, with two
hundred men, should surprise the two out-
lying ships of the enemy. That two of their
own long ships, with their crews made up to
the full number from the trading vessels,
should row out to support him; while the
remainder should get away as fast as they

could before the north-easterly breeze for
Anderida.

A march of about two leagues—three
Roman miles—brought the two hundred to
the hollow between sand-hills described by
Eomaer. The pirates were too busy to
observe them. The crews of the foreign
galleys were scattered abroad, plundering,
burning, ravishing, slaying, and the smoke,
mounting up toward heaven, was borne
away by the wind which rustled the coarse
sea grass.

Eormenred looked to leeward where five
of his vessels with canvas spread were stem-
ming the flood on their homeward voyage.
The two ships, his destined prize, were afloat,
rocking gently on the wide, low waves that
ran up the flat shore, tightening by turns the
landward and the seaward warps.

The Saxons were told off in two groups,
one for each ship, with their swords in the
scabbard, and shields over their shoulders.
The signal was given—away they went at a
round trot, keeping well together, swarmed

over the ships' sides, cut down the score or
so of men they found on board, and the deed
was done—so far at least. Eormenred
cheerfully ordered the shore warps to be cut,
and all hands to clap on to the seaward
ropes.

Alas! the additional weight of a hundred men, about eight tons in each ship,
brought them down in the water so that they
no longer floated.

"Bend your backs, you lazy scoundrels!"
roared Eormenred in a fury, knowing it was
his own fault. "Strength must do it. Now!
all together, with a—Yu-ho-yeoh!"

At the last syllable the ropes parted like
packthread, and two hundred men fell in
heaps among the benches.

"I knew he would do it," said an old sea-
dog, wiping the blood from his nose with the
back of his hand. "I knew he'd do it.
Why didn't ye bring a team of oxen to sea to
pull ye out of your scrapes. Here come
the axes."

The Scandinavians, aroused at last, were

gathering in strength, and the situation was sufficiently awkward. But the danger cooled Eormenred's passion, and stirred up his wits.

" Silence, fore and aft," he cried, " and every man to his station ! Now, all but the men at the oars overboard, and lift the ships off as I give the word, and, oarsmen, pull for your lives ! "

He watched till a wave lifted the bows, the men heaved with a will together, the oars lashed the water into foam, the dripping men scrambled aboard, and the ships floated out of reach of the Scandinavians who followed till the water was up to their necks.

They pulled leisurely out to sea, carefully observing the movements of their enemies. Two of the ships ashore were got off, filled with men, and began rowing furiously after the captured vessels.

" Good," said Eormenred, " we will hoist sail. By the time these fellows are blown we shall be near our two ships, then we will turn and take these, and be ready to fight the rest as they come up. So now you have half an hour to rest before the fun comes."

At the end of half an hour they were near their own galleys, and at the word of command turned upon their pursuers. With a lusty cheer they thrust their own between the enemies' ships, lashed them together, and the fight began.

The Scandinavians, inflamed with the wine they found in the town, and enraged at the loss of their ships, leaped wildly on board, and many fell between the benches and were killed as they struggled to rise. Others were crushed together, and had not room to use their long axes with effect. After a quarter of an hour's sharp fighting the Saxons had cleared their ships of living foemen, and were about to board in their turn, when their consorts came up on the outside, and taking the strangers in the rear, drove them to their half-decks, whence they made deadly play with their axes. With these they held at bay the foemen in front, but fell fast before the darts launched at them from adjacent vessels.

The case seemed desperate, when, with a sudden shock, three fresh ships crashed into the thickest of the fray, the lashings parted— the mass of vessels reeled asunder.

With shouts and frantic cries nearly three hundred fresh warriors leaped on board, headed by Prince Borislav the Wend, and Thorsten the tall, and Gunnur. Then was the hurly-burly of battle—the first shock overthrew many, and once down there was no rising till the business was over, if then. The fallen stabbed and cut with their knives when they could get their arms free from the bleeding writhing heap in each vessel. The merchant seamen, less skilful in the use of their weapons, flung down their swords, drew their knives, and with shouts of "Seax, Seax!" clutched their men by the throat, stabbing savagely underhand. The ships rolled on the heave of the sea, surging together as wind and wave drove them; the combatants fell between them and were crushed or drowned; feet slid in clotted blood, or stumbled among piles of bodies. Tumult and yelling of war-cries, with groans and shrieks of agony, filled the air, but ever in the thickest press swelled the shout, " Seax, Seax!" On the steep hill slopes, shepherds and husbandmen, a peaceful folk, wondered with trembling at the din, the fury. Little leisure had the hovering Wælcyrian to choose the heroes for slaughter. The steam of carnage rose to the nostrils of Woden, who sniffed it with grim approval. Yarl Thorsten was nowhere to be seen. Prince Borislav cleft the skull of Sæbyrht, and wounded Eomaer in the thigh, but Eormenred slashed him across the armpit as he raised his axe, and the Wend bled to death. The ship of Gunnur drifted to leeward, fast grappled with a Saxon, fighting in the gathering darkness. None thought of quarter, and the roaring flame of battle was dying down for lack of fuel, when the squadron sent by Cymen appeared on the scene. A hundred men rushed on board the two leeward ships, and doughty Yarl Bui fell, the last of his crew, with a line of shattered head-pieces in front of him.

Eormenred was fairly the victor before the fresh galleys came up, but their arrival was not the less welcome. He had barely six score men who could stand on their feet, .and of these not a score were without a wound. With so few hands he could not have managed his own two ships and the seven prizes. The new comers towed the nine ashore, where fires were lighted and victuals cooked. Their own men had their hurts dressed roughly, the enemies who still breathed were relieved of their pain, and Eormenred, having posted guards, slept soundly.

The other ships rowed to the still burning town, where they picked up a hundred or so of the outlandish men who had been left behind in the hurry of the embarkation. These being helplessly drunk, were taken on board to row the captured vessels in the morning.

Soon after noon the next day, when the tide turned, the united squadrons launched, and with favouring wind and tide sailed in triumph for Anderida.

CHAPTER IX.

Æ LLE, harassed by the horsemen and archers
of Farinmail, unable to supply himself with
food from his enemy's country, and foreseeing
that he should be obliged to employ half his
army in escorting provision trains, came
quickly to a resolution to transfer his camp
to the sea shore. He chose for its site a
gently rising ground about two miles south
of the camp of the men of Gwent on the
Roman road, and the same distance from
Anderida, from which city it was separated
by salt marshes, covered in most places by
the tide at high water, and intersected by
numerous channels. Here he found an
extensive tract abounding in timber and
pasture, which afforded convenient shelter

for his shipping, and could be isolated by a short trench.

Hither he marched with two thousand chosen men and some trustworthy guides, by the dull radiance of the summer twilight. The force was discovered by British scouts, and beacon fires gave notice of its movements. The garrisons were on the alert, the camp of the men of Gwent was reinforced, and Farinmail's horsemen hung about it, but Ælle wound his way round the hillsides, and passing the intricate country below in the brightening dawn, found himself at his destination soon after sunrise.

The rest of the Saxon army arrived shortly afterwards by sea, and set to work entrenching the position and providing booths for lodging. They also dug wells, but the water was not very good, which gave occasion to these hardy patriots to declare that they would drink beer rather than abandon a camp so well situated.

The summer solstice was now past; three days ago the shadow at noon was at its shortest, and would soon increase by a cock's stride. There were solemnities which could no longer be deferred without imminent risk, for the season was come when dragons would shed on the watersprings seed pestiferous to man and beast, unless driven away by proper rites and suffumigations.

Bale fires, in honour of the sun, had been duly kindled at midsummer, but some of the practices used from time unsearchable had been postponed in consequence of the war.

For these reasons, Ælle determined to hallow his new camp with unusual pomp, and to combine with this ceremony sacrifices to Freá the beneficent. He had told the priests to provide themselves with all things needful, and had given them a hogshead of bright ale, and a hogshead of mead, · and thirty marks of silver by weight. Also he gave three boars to be offered to Freá, one for the blessing of the camp boundary that he would guard it, and one to ensure fertile land and plentiful crops, and one for the increase of their flocks and herds. The great festival of Freá was at Yule, but lesser celebrations occurred at intervals of time, measured by the sacred number, three. Periods of thrice three, and all quantities containing exact nines were esteemed perfectly lucky, therefore the sacrifices were to be made at the ninth hour after noon when the very heavens would be red as if with the blood of the victims.

But when, at the third hour, or a little later, Ælle heard that his squadrons had returned in triumph, bringing with them as prizes seven long ships, and these taken from no contemptible foe, he rejoiced greatly. He thought it well to honour also Tiw, the one-handed war-god, the giver of victory, and his own especial protector; for Ælle was not of the race of Woden.

He left his officers to carry on the works both for defence and feasting, and stepping into Sæfugl was rowed quickly across to the point where the fleet lay, accompanied by Ostrythe and Eanfled, and others followed with everything they used for dressing wounds.

When the king came to the place, he called Eormenred, heard the story of the fight, and praised him much; but when it was told him that out of four hundred men, one hundred and twenty-two were killed, and one hundred and fifty so badly hurt that they could not stand on their feet, he laughed and said—

"So should men die. They feast with the heroes."

Then he visited the wounded whom the seamen had brought ashore and laid in their own huts. Ælle spoke kindly to each, and this won him much love though he was a hard man. He bid the sailors build a long booth open to the south, where the wounded might lie covered from sun and rain, enjoying the cool sea breeze.

All of the four hundred who could come the king bid to his feast that night, but many preferred to rest, for their hurts were stiff, though not disabling. To all he promised due rewards, but to Eomaer he said that he would give him arms.

Then Ælle examined the prisoners, one hundred and seven in number, and among them was Thorsten the tall. Staggered with drink, he had fallen unwounded, and was soon covered with dead and dying. After the battle he was found still breathing though well-nigh smothered, and was recognised as a chief by the splendour of his armour. The king immediately picked him out as one of the three to be sacrificed to the war-god, but Thorsten had been beforehand with him. He had bought the friendship of Brihthelm, a sea captain, by discovering to him a secret hoard of silver. As soon therefore as they came to land, they swore brotherhood in the usual fashion. In the presence of twelve witnesses Thorsten and Brihthelm cut each of them a turf and covered his head with it. Then each made incision of his arm, and letting their blood mingle in a goblet of wine, they drank the mixture with tremendous imprecations.

Brihthelm now claimed his brother, Thorsten became Ælle's man, and another victim
was found for Tiw.

By this it was time to return, for the sun
had fallen behind the western hills, and the
hour of sacrifice was at hand.

The priests had set up an altar for Tiw,
a broad, flat stone, resting on two others
planted edgewise, and had chosen a fitting
place for a Friths-plot, and they hallowed
these and also a thorn for Tiw. They had
moreover erected an altar for Freá, which
was built partly of turf, and a ledge of turf
encompassed it that the blood of the victims
might not be spilt on the ground. This also
they hallowed.

In the midst of the Friths-plot, where the
ground rose gently, was a great heap of wood
with dry reeds, and a pitch barrel on the
weather side. When the king landed, the
chief priest was kindling pure fire by rubbing
two sticks together, and the priest was stout
and the afternoon hot, but at length he was
successful. Then he announced that the

ninth hour was come, and set fire to the reeds, and the flames roared, fanned by the sea wind. As the bonfire burnt up, bones were cast into it, and offal and filth of all sorts, and a horrible stench arose, and scared away the dragons from all that country.

Then they compassed the fire thrice, moving with the sun, and rolling with them a wheel, signifying thereby that the luminary had reached the highest point of his coúrse and must return. Then they snatched brands from the fire, and danced round the pile, with songs and indescribable gestures, still turning with the sun.

When this was accomplished, the king, accompanied by the priests and all the people, bent their steps in solemn procession to the altar of Freá, the god of plenty. This deity was, perhaps, more regarded than any. Woden was terrible, but Woden was not always successful. Tiw was valiant and the giver of valour; they respected the hardihood of him, who, for sufficient cause, thrust his hand into the wolf's mouth, knowing that it would be bitten off, nevertheless brave men, trusting in their own might and main, could get on very well without Tiw. But the husbandman knows that his toil is vain unless seconded by seasonable heat and moisture, and that the health and fruitfulness of flocks and herds is in many particulars beyond his control. There was therefore no want of attention in the people standing before Freá's altar when the priest, lifting toward heaven the sacrificial knife, and laying his left hand on the mighty boar, which lay bound on the altar, sang in monotonous voice :

Freá ! Freá ! Freá !
Giver of fertility,
In heaven sitting
By the high hearth,
Hear us singing
The spell of sooth.

By the triple charm,
By tree, turf, and blood,
Thick may the grass grow
In the green meadow,
Fruitful the field be,
Fruitful the orchard,
Send us the sunshine
And shower in due season.

Shedding the boar's blood,
Bowing we bid thee,
Thee, the Field-Father !
Freá ! Freá ! Freá !

Men bent their heads in unfeigned devotion as the priest struck his broad blade into the boar's throat; what they asked for was of vital importance to them, and they believed that Freá could grant it. The chief priest dipped an ash branch in the blood, and sprinkled the earth and a basket of corn and fruit, and cast some drops up toward the sky. Then the boar was removed, and his entrails examined to ascertain the prospect of the crops of the year, and after that he was roasted at a fire made of ash boughs and billets, because that wood burns readily in a green state.

The second boar was slain in the same manner, but Freá was invoked for the horses and kine, sheep, and other animals, that they might increase and be healthy, and give abundance of milk, wool, and other produce.

The third sacrifice, for blessing the boundaries, was managed differently. The saturated turf was pierced, and the blood, caught in bronze vessels, was carried round the camp, and sprinkled all about the rampart and ditch, and the place where the gate should be.

Red were the fires on the altar of Tiw, making the thin, sharp crescent-moon, now low in the west, appear more pale and beautiful. The people and the thorn tree were sprinkled with the blood of horses and other victims, and the flesh being roasted, the choicest portions were reserved for the king's table. Fresh fuel was heaped on, till the broad altar-stone sent forth a quivering heat, and the quick element devoured the parts assigned to it, while thick fat smoke, with trains of sparks, incensed the sacred thorn. A boy, whose meagreness exaggerated the size of his head and joints, was brought to the priests by his father and kinsmen to be cured of an evil spirit, which possessed him in consequence of his having been ill-wished. The father, a dull, heavy man of property, who had not brains enough for the apprehension of danger, explained that an old hag, whose son he happened to kill, had filled the lad with a spirit of cowardice. He had taken the witch before the tything-men, and as she would neither confess nor reverse the spell, she suffered the penalty of the law. The priest bid the father bring the lad, with proper offerings to the altar of Tiw, and the charm would be removed. So one led forward a young horse to be sacrificed, and each of the kinsmen offered a gift, according to his degree, that the disgrace of cowardice might be taken away from the family. The servants of Tiw said that it was a simple matter to cure the defect, but added that the ardent breath of the god sometimes absorbed the life of the patient. The father answered that it were better to die than to live in shame. Then the lad, who had been dazed by the unwonted scene, began to cry, but they buffeted him till he held his peace.

His screams were renewed when he was stripped and smeared with the blood of the horse, and wrapped in its newly flayed skin. The heart and entrails of the victim were cast into the fire, and as the reek ascended, the boy, enveloped in the skin, was dragged backwards and forwards through the hollow place formed by the side stones and top of the altar. The shrieks ceased by degrees, and the priests announced that the cure was complete.

The king feasted in the open air, when the rites were concluded, and the chief men sat on benches, which together with the tables, had been brought from the booth of the Gesithas at Wlencing; and those of the guests for whom there were no seats sat on the grass. Cymen, in spite of his bruises, took the end of one table, while Cissa presided at another; but Ælle was in the middle of the cross table, with Eormenred on his right hand.

The goodman of the Old House had conquered the prejudice of the sea captains, who could not resist the claim of such a bloody victory. The host had supped abundantly on the cattle and sheep, the produce of the foray, and praised Eormenred over the drink which the king's liberality afforded them. Torches blazed smokily over the coarse banquet, revealing some points of religious cookery which might well have been concealed.

When all had eaten and drunk enough they rose, and most men went to their sleeping quarters ; but a group gathered around the king and Eormenred, greedy for details of the fighting, which the hero of the day told with sufficient bluntness. When this topic was exhausted the talk languished, till Cymen observed—

"When these seven fresh ships are manned we ought to make an effort. I am not prepared at present to say what ; but something should be done."

" I will have nothing attempted," Ælle said, " without my knowledge and leave obtained."

"There is one thing," Cissa remarked, "which ought to be done at once, and it would not be very difficult or very hazardous. That long bridge should be broken down—destroyed; then we could take the city and the army singly, and deal more easily with both."

"True," said Ælle; "but how are we to overcome the obstacles which bar the water-way?"

"Let the obstructions be carefully noted at low water with reference to certain fixed objects ashore, then, at high water spring tide, small boats may be guided between them, or rafts floated over them. Many men are not needed; fire will do the work if we can prevent it being too soon extinguished."

"The matter is worth consideration, but we must not talk of it in public, or the enemy will hear it. I think the air and the winds betray our counsels."

The party broke up, and shortly afterwards Bael wriggled from under a bush and glided away in a coracle.

CHAPTER X.

The sea breeze brought up clouds with sunrise, and rain was falling steadily as Julius, with four followers, rode over the long bridge. As soon as the destination of the Saxon host was assured, he had marked out a camp which should contract, within narrow limits, their power of annoyance on the landward side. A range of low hills ran in a southerly direction from the camp of the men of Gwent to within half a mile of Ælle's trench. On the most commanding point of this range, the engineers had laid out a fortification overlooking the flats on either side, and gangs of men relieved each other, working day and night on the defences. Julius had been keeping the people to their work, snatching an hour's repose at intervals, and was now returning to his duties in the city.

Half-way across the bridge, Bael clambered up by the piles, and Julius, perceiving from his face that he was laden with tidings, checked his horse, and desired the attendants to ride forward. Bael had a fancy that the bridge was a good place for telling secrets, as he could assure himself that no one was at hand to listen ; but he was in full view from the walls and other places, and it is certain that the first point in the art of concealment is to hide the fact that there is anything to conceal. Julius humoured the weakness, though he knew that a more private spot would have been safer, and heard Bael's report then and there. After so doing, he studied for some minutes the land beyond the bridge, on the seaward side, appeared to come to a conclusion, and moved forward, Bael walking at his stirrup.

" What would be the best way for a party of four," he asked, "two of them women, unable for much exertion, to get to the edge of the forest at the foot of Pen y Coit, without attracting attention ? "

" Light boat from here two hours, horses one hour, boat two hours, horse half an hour, boat two hours. Mad fellow often goes."

" Then there are horses and boats at the proper points."

" Yes; but I don't know if the boats would hold two women."

" If the mad fellow wished to manage it he would find no difficulty."

" He has no difficulties. Devils help him; great magic he knows."

" Well, keep about here, for I may want you suddenly. The reasons——"

" Never mind the reasons. Say what you want short and clear, so as to be easily remembered. Don't muddle me with reasons."

" Very well," answered Julius, "and do you the same if you want aught."

By this time they had reached the Forum, and Julius entered his house, where he sent for one official and desired him to draw certain plans for which he gave sufficient directions; of another he ordered building material to be obtained from the ruined houses of the city; from a third he required workmen. He was about to build a tower on the southern side of the bridge head, for the better protection of the work there, and of the boom which floated on the seaward side of the bridge, within the sunken ships.

Meanwhile rain poured down steadily from the gloomy sky. Bronwen, with several slaves about her, and the necessary toilet arrangements, sat with a bright steel mirror in her hand, in the room from which Ostrythe had departed with little ceremony. The lattice window was open for light and air, and the rain drove in, the drops splashing with aggravating persistence. The slaves suffered for the fault of the weather. Fotis had dressed her lady's head twenty times, and the tunic hanging in rags from her girdle, the red marks on her shoulders, and her ruffled hair, bore witness with what ill-success. Again Bronwen consulted her mirror, again was dissatisfied, and vented her vexation on the slave.

" Kneel ! " cried the petulant child, " bend your body more."

Bronwen struck several blows with the back of the mirror, but her arm was too feeble for the due punishment of the fault.

" I will have her scourged," she said, " send for the——"

At this moment there was a tap at the chamber door, and Narses being introduced, made obeisance with all humility, saying—

" There is a man in the court, one of the religious, who seeks the favour of a brief conference with the Lady Bronwen."

" Ah ! " sighed Bronwen lazily, "what manner of man is he ? "

" He is tall, thin, dressed in a coarse woollen frock with a leathern girdle, from which hangs a gourd, and he carries a pilgrim staff."

" But his face ? " she exclaimed pettishly. " Is he young or old ? "

"Middle-aged I guess from his gait; but his face is covered by his hood, and his voice has a strange foreign tone."

"If he have travelled far he may amuse us. Admit him."

Narses, who belonged to the secret society, pretended not to be acquainted with its chief, that Bronwen's curiosity might be excited about him.

Renatus entered after a brief delay. His salutation had a hollow ring in it, and he cast a curious glance around from under the shadow of his hood. He noted the ill-ordered luxury, the shabby splendour, the copy of a copy of magnificence. He saw the livid marks on Fotis's naked shoulders, and scanned the lines of Bronwen's face with an emotion which held him silent. Years had elapsed since he last saw her—a tender, dark-eyed creature, who stole into his heart in his own despite with trustful looks and broken music of childish words. Then she claimed his pity, for the shadow and the stain were cast upon her by others; but now, surrounded with the tawdry pomp of a petty court, his natural repugnance was reinforced by the evidence of her selfishness and cruelty. He was startled by the hardness of the voice which cried to him—

" Have you anything to say, or are you an image for us to admire ? "

Renatus roused himself, and answered sternly—

" Send away these creatures—these slaves."

"At your command, no indeed. You have too much the air of an assassin. Speak, if you have any matter to speak of, before my maidens ; if you have nothing to say, leave us."

" I will do as you desire. Wandering in the night to meditate without distraction, I chanced to pass a narrow lane, and from the terrace of the building above came the voice of one singing to the harp. A light was shown for an instant, a ladder was pushed across the lane, and a young man walked on it from terrace to terrace. Fearing that a robbery or some mischief was on hand——"

"What is all this to me?" asked Bronwen languidly. "However, it occurs to me that there is something I could tell you about that affair. Leave us." The slaves departed, and their mistress said, "Go on with the story."

"Suspecting that all was not right, I entered the garden to which the terrace looked, and there, under a pergula—a trellis, covered by a luxuriant vine, in the corner farthest from the door——"

"It is false!" exclaimed Bronwen, turning crimson and starting to her feet; "a wicked lie; and your life is forfeit for intruding there!"

"I was not really there, but as it were in a dream or vision."

"Why do you tell me such rubbish?" she said in her confusion.

"Well, it is true, as none knows better than yourself, but I will not speak of the matter as it displeases you; indeed, the subject on which I desired to confer with you is totally different."

" I am ready to hear you, only do not be too long in telling it."

" Strange histories are poured into the ears of religious men by such as need the consolations of religion, and what is freely confessed to them they will rather die than reveal. One life sheds light upon another, and so it comes about that they know more of a man or woman than he or she knows of the past, the future, or even the present course of each. You are lonely here."

"Lonely, yes; and sometimes—oh, so weary."

" Have you ever wondered, sought to know the reason of the isolation which causes this tedium—this weariness."

" No. It seems inevitable, part of myself. Even in my earliest years I seem to remember the same sensation hanging over me."

"Can you remember much of that early time ? Surely your fancy must darken the picture. In those innocent days what grief or trouble could vex your spirit ? Tell me of that time, as much of it as has not faded from your memory. Perhaps, seeking in the past, we may find a remedy for the grief of the present."

" I could fancy I remember your voice," said Bronwen, " as you speak now. It sounded quite differently at first."

" Tell me what is the first thing you recollect—the very first."

" It must have been at Calleva."* Bronwen spoke very slowly—"I have an impression of a bright day, and many people sitting in rows, some of them small, like dolls. The people shouted, and down below, in the pit covered with sand, the sun flashed on bright armour, so bright I could scarcely bear to look on it. Suddenly there was greater noise and confusion, and the people stood up on the seats, and my nurse stood and raised me in her arms. Then I saw a man without armour down below, who held up a cross and spoke very loud. Then we were in a dark passage and on stairs, with a sound of many

* Silchester.

feet trampling heavily overhead, and screaming all around, and suddenly we were in the
sunshine again. After that, soon after I
think, a light shone on my eyes and I opened
them, and saw on one side nurse with a
lamp, and on the other the man who held
up the cross, and his eyes were like coals of
fire. He said, ' Poor child!' and they went
away."

Renatus put his hand to his head, and
said, after a pause—

" Your memory is good. What else does
it retain ? "

" The next thing is less distinct, but I see
more than I can describe. We were travelling in a wood, we had been travelling a long
time, but the wood was endless. By-and-
by it grew dark, but I knew we were going
on still. When we stopped I awoke, and
saw torches near at hand and torches beyond, and men were calling from beyond,
and a man on our side answered. Presently
there was a shock, and men fell, and horses,
and torches waved hither and thither. While

I looked at them something bright gleamed down on us, and nurse fell, still holding me, and the warm blood ran over my face. I never saw my nurse again. I used to wake in the night and cry for her, and they beat me. After that all is confused till I came here."

" When did that happen ? "

" It was before the battle of Mercredes-burn ; that is not what they called it then— I forget ;—but I remember the messenger bringing the news of the fight, and that my father sent me a silver serpent armlet, and I wore it on my ankle. It must have been years before that I came ; for a long time he took no notice of me, but after his return I saw him daily when he was at the palace."

" You have told me nothing of your mother."

" I know nothing about her. I have no recollection whatever of her; but I have heard people speak of her in my presence when they thought me too young to under-stand or remember, and their remarks have left the impression that she died unhappily."

" May it not be that this sadness, which you say has always oppressed you, had its origin in the want of a mother's care ? "

" What could my mother have done more than my nurse did ?   She loved me very dearly, I remember that, and I loved her."

" The difference cannot be told.   It is like life itself, an essence too subtle for words, and only to be fully understood by those who have known it, and prized it—and lost it. To me," Renatus continued, with a tremor in his voice, which was very low and tender, " to me, full of years and full of sorrows, bending under a load too heavy for life and reason—to any man alive—what but the love of a mother in the past could give assurance of the love of God now and hereafter ; a love which is boundless, which unasked gives all, seeking only love in return.   From rest in the arms of our mother, to the rest in the embrace of death, all is weariness, bitterness, and sin.   Nothing earthly can compare with a mother's love, nothing can replace it— nothing—nothing."

Neither spoke for a minute ; then Bronwen asked with a sigh—

"Why do you tell me this ? Why dwell on the surpassing value of the treasure, when it is lost beyond recall ? Will you cure the ache by showing the remedy, and bidding the sufferer despair of obtaining it ? "

" I do not give pain for the sake of giving pain. I would open to your mind a view beyond your present experience, and give you an opportunity of judging things, motives, duties, by a higher standard than any you have yet tried. I have shown you this love, so true, so generous ; is it not to be prized for its intrinsic, its unalienable beauty and sweetness ? Should the object of such affection presume to slight it, because through some accident or fault the loving heart has been denied the privilege of expressing itself in word or action ? If you were judge in such a case, would you not deem that daughter base and ungrateful, who, having it in her power to satisfy a dying mother's wish, refused through sloth and selfishness to indulge it—a wish of easy accomplishment at small cost to herself—a wish that reached no higher than once to see that child of her love ?　Would you not condemn such a daughter ? "

" I suppose so ; but whereto does all this tend ? "

" The case I lay before you is no imaginary one.　The mother exists, the daughter exists ; it rests in your power to decide whether maternal love and filial piety shall have one sad last occasion of mutual endearment."

" I apprehend that it is for one of my slaves you plead.　Less circumstance might have sufficed ; I am not such a harsh mistress as to require so much mollifying.　Tell me her name, and if she be not altogether un-worthy of indulgence, the boon is granted, not grudgingly, but with pleasure."

" She is not unworthy," Renatus replied, " though through want of guidance she may have gone astray ; nor is she a slave, save in so far as none is free who is mastered by passion.　The daughter, Lady Bronwen, is

yourself, the mother is your own. For her
I plead, not, oh I am sure, not in vain. A
fault—nay, I will not extenuate anything, a
grievous deadly sin, separated her from the
world and from you ; from you—that was the
sharpest point of anguish, the rest could be
endured. She lavished on lazars and lepers
the loving care she could not bestow on you.
Now, worn out with penitence, with works
of charity, with the unappeased yearning of
her heart, she craves the sight of you for
one short hour. You cannot, you will not
refuse her."

" My mother," said Bronwen, frightened,
" it cannot be, after so many years ! What
assurance have I that this is true ? "

" Your memory is good, and I will trust to
it." Renatus turned back his hood—" You
have seen this face before, poor child ? "

" The man with the cross," Bronwen
whispered ; " I remember you. What am I
to do ? Where must I go ? My father, will
he—— "

But Renatus showed an order signed by

the Count, and countersigned by the Praefect, the . contents of which Bronwen did not quite understand ; he anticipated objections, smoothed all difficulties, and finally, by force of will, prevailed.

CHAPTER XI.

WITH laughter and song and favouring breeze
three ships ran down the coast westaway,
bearing the jolly Saxons to their fields.
Though a restless, wander-foot race, none
surpass them in love of home and homely
joys. Now they were bound to their wives
and bairns, they would tread their own acres,
the sithe would swing in their hard hands,
sweeping down swathes of thick grass.
Eormenred admitted to himself that the land
clave to him more than it should if the sea-
dogs were right; and as with him so was it
with his comrades, all bound for home as
blithe as children.

Ælle sent home the three ships whose
crews had borne the brunt of the late en-
gagement, that the wounded might recruit

their strength, not perhaps without a hope that the stories they told might draw fresh men to fill up the vacancies in the ranks. He had found it necessary to send back many of those who had flocked to him after his defeat. His position was now secure from attack, and there were some of his old warriors whose will was better than their power, some who were really more useful in their villages than with the host.

Eormenred stood on the poop of his ship, and near him lay his wounded son, drinking in renewed strength with every breath of sea air. He was weak and wan, quite unable to walk, but full of spirit, talking of seeing his mother again.

" You will let me tell her, will you not, father ? "

" Tell her what ? How you jumped the ditch, or how you came by that chop in the thigh ? You may tell her."

" No, no ! I would rather you said all that. I mean that the king spoke to me, promised to give me arms."

"Why are you so glad to be a Gesith? Would you not rather stay with the mother, and help me with the ploughing, and the mowing, and the reaping, and the shearing? Would not that be better?"

" I will, father, if you bid me."

But Eormenred desired it as little as his son, and said, laughing—

" No, no, lad; you shall tell the mother that you are a man and a Gesith, honoured and rewarded by Ælle the King. There are enough to do the work without you, and you shall begin for yourself. After harvest, when you have got your allotment, we and our kinsfolk will come for a se'nnight or more, and help you to build house and barn and to break up the new land. My share of the plunder will come to something this year, you shall have part of it, as well as your own, to stock the farm, and we will set you up bravely. I will not fail to tell the mother how you came to your father's side when his shield was broken and three axes hung over his head. Mildred shall make a song of it,

and he shall sing of the sea-fight also. I will
give him a cow if he does it well."

Tears stood in the boy's eyes as he kissed
the rough hand which rested on his head.
Eormenred went on with newly fledged
pride—

" We who are admitted to share the king's
secret counsels, know that this war will soon
be at an end, though I am not at liberty to
point out the means to be employed to finish
it. Afterwards there will be a season of
peace, to settle and strengthen ourselves
before we make a push northerly. Then in
a few years you will quit the Gesithas to
marry a good helpful lass, and have free land
of your own, and stout sons to stand by you
as you have stood by me."

So they talked, and the morning waned.
One ship ran into the Adur river, but Eormenred with the others held on till they came
to Arun mouth, where at a settlement of the
Tortingas, two leagues up the stream, they
drew the long ships ashore and covered them
with boughs and old sails to protect them

from the weather till it was time to return.
The wounded who belonged to the neigh-
bouring Marks found means of conveyance,
and Eormenred took boats and proceeded up
the river with his fellowship.

The river wound its way between hills and
woods, and they pulled slowly against the
sluggish stream, with tracts of flag and bog-
bean, asphodel, orchis, and marsh-marigold
in the loops on either hand. They passed
between the chalk hills, came out on the
northern side of the barrier, and landed
about a league further on, where a large
brook runs in from the westward. They cut
willow branches, weaving the twigs together,
and made comfortable litters on which to
carry the wounded.

The land on both sides was in their own
Mark, the original beech and oak forest, rich
and productive when brought under cultiva-
tion. From the woodland they passed into
waterside meadows, where long stretches of
grass stood awaiting the mower, and on the
left a steep bank in which tree roots writhed

like tangled serpents amid hollows filled with
moss and ferns and sloping spikes of purple
foxglove. Between bushes, almost veiled in
traveller's joy, just coming into bloom, were
to be had glimpses of green downs, dotted
with cattle diminishing in the distance, and
sheep grazing between clumps of trees
interspersed with gnarled thorns and stiff
junipers.

As the track wound upward farmsteads
appeared, the buildings constructed chiefly of
timber, or of timber frames filled in with
chalk or clay. The fields were long fenceless
strips of corn and pulse, with furlongs of
fallow intervening.

The nucleus of the Mark was a group of
houses by the stream, now much reduced in
size ; the mill and the smithy stood on one
side of an open space shaded in its centre by
a venerable tree, and on another side was the
house of Tota the priest, also a shop for the
sale of necessaries not produced in the neighbourhood, and a sort of open shed for certain
public purposes.

All the population appeared to be clustered
round the great tree, under which was the
seat of justice, the concourse and the attention
of the audience testifying the interest taken
in the proceedings. As the long procession,
with many litters, wound between the buildings, it was discovered by a troop of urchins,
who recognised Eormenred, and immediately
scampered off to spread the news of his
arrival. But the matter for consideration
under the spreading oak boughs was too
serious to be interrupted, and the crowd
made way for Eormenred to take his seat
on the bench. The litters were borne to
the dwellings of the wounded men, whose
relatives followed and attended to their
wants; those who had helped to bring the
boats and litters from the Mark of the
Totingas being paid and dismissed.

The crowd in front of the tything-men
consisted chiefly of women, many of them in
a state of great excitement, talking volubly.
The eldest of the tything-men, one Ealdhelm, explained the progress of the suit to

the new comer, saying that it was not a
question of fact, but of law.

Gurhan was on his trial for excessive and
illegal beating of his wife Wulflaed. The
wife, besides being a busybody, a scold, a
neglecter of her children and household, had
filled up the vessel of her husband's wrath
by failing to have food ready for him when
he returned from the field, and when she
counselled him to cook for himself, it over-
flowed with reproaches. Finding that words
were of no avail—were indeed flung back with
more than equal vivacity—the husband proceeded, with sorrow of heart as he said, to
correct her with a stick, fragments of which
were before the court.

Wulflaed replied with much acrimony that
her husband was naught. That he feigned
sickness to avoid going to the war. That
when he went abroad it was not to work in
the field but to drink with any who would
give him drink, and to flirt with wenches, of
whom she named two, namely, Hild the black
and Eahswith ; whereupon a terrible clamour

arose, and the tything-men could not still it for a long time. At last silence was restored, and the law-men declared that all this matter was beside the point. Gurhan had undoubted right to chastise his wife if she were unruly, the law having foreseen the necessity, and ordained that the stick used should be of a certain thickness, to wit, the size of a man's thumb.

Thereupon, Wulflaed made a fresh outcry that Gurhan used sticks of uncertain thickness, to wit, the first that came to hand ; and moved the court to have the stick measured, and also her husband's thumb, to ascertain whether it were a lawful stick or no.

Upon measurement, the stick was found to exceed the thumb by one-third part of a barley-corn, and judgment was about to be given, when Gurhan, who had been busy with a string, cried out—

" The law says, as big as a man's thumb ; here is a man, namely, Sprow the miller, whose thumb exceeds the bigness of the stick by half a barley-corn."

Then Wulflaed opened her mouth and cried in a shrill, sustained voice that made the ears tingle, saying, that the husband's thumb was the natural, customary, and lawful thumb, and she would stand or fall by it and by no other; that Sprow's thumb was an unnatural and unhallowed enlargement, an engine of fraud and covetise ; and she proceeded to curse Sprow, his parents, his children, all millers, and mankind in general, in words so abundant and stinging, that few men marvelled to hear of her husband using sticks of uncertain thickness.

At the last she had to be gagged and bound, and the tything-men having conferred together, Ealdhelm spoke in the name of all -

" The thickness of the husband's thumb is mostly taken as the fit size of a stick to chasten his wife withal. But in any case of disputed measurement the standard is reckoned by the king's body, and parts thereof, as his arm or foot. Undoubtedly therefore the king's thumb is the measure of the lawful stick. But when the king is not present, nor any known measure of his thumb, nor any means of speedily getting the same, it has been, and is customary and lawful, to take the standard from the eldest lawman present, that one who pronounces the doom of the rest—I am that man."

While the lawful thumb was being measured, the others talked.

" This Gurhan should be declared nithing, however this may turn out," said one; "Ælle will be ill pleased if he hear of it."

" For not going to host," said another; " but he is no good in war or peace."

"Gurhan is a fool and parcel knave, and should be punished to deter such fellows from shirking duty," was Eormenred's opinion, "but as regards the stick, a good blackthorn, or an ashen stick of half the size, would do more work than this soft stuff."

The stick was unlawful, and the law-men having consulted together came quickly to a decision, and their doom, spoken by Ealdhelm was, that neither husband nor wife was any better than he or she should be, and that unless they mended their way without loss of time, the hand of the law would be heavy upon them. That the stick was no lawful stick, and that Gurhan was to pay one silver groat, to be laid out in Scot-ale for the refreshment of the officials when next they met to take counsel for the common weal, Gurhan being kept in bonds, without light, food, or drink, till the money was paid. That Gurhan should be thankful that such a lenient view was taken of his offence, which was due partly to the merciful disposition of his judges, and partly to their conviction that it would be difficult, if not impossible, to get more out of him.

Ealdhelm furthermore gave notice, that it would be necessary to hold a meeting for public business at once.

"The body of our good neighbour and tything-man, Sæbyrht, slain in the late sea-fight, has been brought home by his kin and friends for burial. The rites to be practised on such occasions are matters of priest-craft,

therefore, if it seem well to you, we will meet
at the house of Tota, hard by here."

Gurhan then promised that if freed from
bonds he would bring a Scot-ale to the house
of Tota, so sweet, so bright, and such good
measure, that the demands of justice should
be abundantly satisfied, and this was allowed.

After that Eormenred mounted on a bench,
and told in few and sad terms the story of
the fight. The fifty men from this early-
settled and flourishing Mark had fought like
bulldogs round their neighbour and leader ;
not one flinched ; there was glory enough.
Ælle the King had said that he never knew
anything better done. Then he had to tell
it :—Nineteen were killed, twelve lay in the
booths by Anderida who could not be moved
but would probably recover, fifteen wounded
he had brought home, and four besides himself were unscathed. Eighteen would return
no more to plough and sow and reap harvest ;
the Wælcyrian had chosen them to feast with
the heroes ; they lay far away by the shore of
the sea, but they would not be forgotten—all

would be honoured in the burial of Sæbyrht. Then he spoke of the dead by name, relating the exploits of each, and how he fell.

Eormenred ceased, and there was a deep silence; men heard the bubbling of the brook as it ran its course; and far away, bleating of sheep and lowing of cattle coming home from the hills. Twilight was deepening; already it was dark under the great oak; and the meeting melted away like a sunset cloud.

Eomaer meanwhile was carried up to his father's house, which stood apart. It was a vast structure, in which the present tenants could scarcely be said to dwell; they lurked like lizards in a desolate palace. The outer walls, now overgrown and ruinous, except where they served as night quarters for the swine, enclosed a space of nearly five acres, chiefly orchard ground. Fragments of mosaic work, of marbles and fine pottery, were scattered about between the moss-grown trunks. Within this enclosure stood a quadrangle of buildings differing in height and in their state of preservation; some showed marks

of fire, some of dilapidation due to the hand
of time, some had been partially pulled down
to afford material for rude repairs of other
parts. In times not long passed away, it
must have been a splendid and sumptuous
abode ; now it was occupied by barbarians
and their animals. Within the quadrangle
was a garden, which, under the supervision
of a slave whose grandfather had cultivated
the soil for a Roman master, showed some
signs of skill and taste.

Eomaer was borne in past a long range
of rooms—painted halls heaped up with grain ;
chambers where cattle stood on rich mosaic
pavements—past the baths, a part of which
was converted into a malting-house—to a
wide colonnade, whose pavement was cum-
bered with heaps of stone and plaster, broken
shafts, and fallen capitals. By a mound of
rubbish his mother stood, shading her eyes
from the oblique sunbeams. Beautiful was
the light on the hills, but she gazed not on
their hazy glory, she looked to see if the kine
were descending, for milking time was at

hand. She strained her eyes to where the Roman way sloped like a baldric across the breast of the down; her ears were filled with farmyard noises, and she heeded not the stir behind her, till a well-known voice was heard saying—

"Will you not look at me, mother?"

She turned, and the same glance which showed her son, revealed also that he was wounded—seriously wounded. She indulged in no hysterical ebullitions, which pertain rather to selfishness than to true love, but kissed him tenderly twice and thrice, asking—

"Is the father hurt?"

While the boy was yet answering she sent her maidens for water, and linen, and simples, and proceeded to search the wound. It was healing kindly, so she washed him and combed his hair, made a couch for him on the tesselated pavement, screening him warily from the sun; she fetched cool buttermilk to slake his thirst, and sat on a low stool holding his hand while he said his say—

"The king came to the hut and asked how

old I was. 'Seventeen winters,' I answered. He was silent for a minute, and then said, 'I have no Gesith as young as that, but I shall make you one;' then he added, 'And I wish I could get a hundred more of such stuff as you are.' It is not boasting to tell it to you, mother, is it?"

The red kine lowed; the swine came routing home with multitudinous grunting and squealing; but Geatflæd heard nothing of it all. So they sat with question and answer, the shadows lengthening till all was shade, and clear stars stood above the hills. Then Eormenred came in, and all gathered about him—free labourers and serfs, and their families. Tables were laid under the colonnade and they supped, and when the meal was ended, Eormenred told all the story again. The children stood round and wondered, but Eostrewine looked discontented, and longed to have a share in such deeds till Eomaer beckoned to him, and having brought his brother to his side, whispered—

" The king gives me new arms, and the

father says you are to have the old harness
and arms, all except the seax, which he says
he will keep, You will take my place now,
and help the father, and go to the war when
you are called. I need not bid you be brave ;
but be steady, and vex not the dear mother."

"Never fear for me. I know how to
behave," said Eostrewine.

"The next day Eormenred was up with
the sun. He rode over his land, inspected
his stock, looked into everything, praised one,
rebuked another. He went to the meadows
with his sithe, and led the mowers till dinner-
time came with abundance of meat and beer.

After the mid-day meal the procession was
formed to take Sæbyrht's body to the burial.
The freemen of the Mark carried the bier
by turns, and the tything-men and others
followed, among them three men of the
children of Beorlaf, who were akin to
Sæbyrht's widow and to Geatflaed. Before
the bier marched Tota the priest, and Mildred the song-smith ; the former chanting
the praises of the gods, the latter reciting

the brave and worthy deeds of him whom they desired to honour ; and between these two a horse was led.

Tota was but lightly esteemed; he had been known to ride a stallion and to bear arms, and do other things unpriest-like ; on the other hand he sang well, and had wondrous strong charms to heal ailments of man or beast. It was whispered that he could inflict harms as well as cure them. Altogether he was well enough. The best men among the Saxons loved fighting and farming better than to be priests, and mutter spells.

The line slowly ascended the stone-paved road, but turned off at the hill top and crossed the grass to where a pit, four feet deep, had been dug in the chalk. Here they laid Sæbyrht's body, clad in armour, and with his weapons as he fell. The horse was slain with due observance, while the priest sang Tiw's hymn. The widow laid on her husband's breast her choicest ornament—a necklace of amber beads from the Baltic

shore; some threw in coins; some placed
meat and drink, some implements for hunting or fishing, beside him. Then, while they
filled the pit, and piled a cairn above it, Tota
sang the glories of Woden's hall, the fighting,
the feasting, the flashing-eyed Shieldmays,
and when the rites were done, the people
dispersed.

Eormenred, with Bosa and the two other
sons of Beorlaf, went with the widow to her
home, to arrange what should be done concerning Sæbyrht's property. About his free
land in the Mark there was no doubt or
difficulty; it had been given by lot to him
and his sons for ever, on conditions of military service and the construction and repair
of roads, bridges, and strongholds. But besides this, Sæbyrht had acquired a hide of
folkland, in the neighbourhood of his wife's
kinsmen, and had cleared and cultivated it.
At his death, this slice of the common-land
went back to the community which had
granted it. Acres were abundant, and
Sæbyrht's deserts great, and it was thought

the freemen might be induced to re-grant this hide to the second son on easy terms.

Afterwards Eormenred took his wife's kinsmen to the villa, where Geatflæd received them in the portico, and offered the drink of welcome. Some of the vapid dulness which earned for their father the name of Beorlaf—flat beer—still lingered about these men, though tempered by a brisker strain of blood derived from their mother. By means of another judicious cross, their children were endued with as much liveliness as is usual among Saxons; and their descendants on the South-Saxon hills are not observed to be flatter than their neighbours. Eormenred led his visitors to a handsome room, paved with mosaic patterns. One represented a boy carried by an eagle; another was a large circle filled with dancing girls. Here Eomaer lay on a rude couch, and each Beorlafing kissed him and spoke a few kindly words. The tables were laid, and smoking dishes placed on them, which made boards bend and tressels crack.

Meats and cookery were alike heroic. Masses of boiled pork, such as delight the warriors in the hall of Woden; lumps of sacrificial horse-flesh, half burnt, half raw; dark, ponderous loaves containing scattered fragments of millstone; mead, ale, and cider, in greasy leathern jugs; such were the viands, and the seats were three-legged stools.

The shade of the fastidious Roman who built the villa, hovering about the scene of former magnificence, floated into the banqueting-hall. He cast one hasty glance around, and fled shuddering back to hell.

But the Saxons were strong fellows who worked hard; their grinders were strong, their ilia hard as those of reapers. They fed like hungry men, and were satisfied.

Bosa, who as the eldest Beorlafing was expected by his brethren to do such talking as could not well be avoided, and had thereby acquired a certain facility of speech, now turned to Geatflæd and said—

" We are glad, kinswoman, and the same to you, Eormenred, and we, Beorlafingas, never

say more than we mean, unless by ill-hap,
which may befall any, as you well know,
Eormenred; for did not the wolves kill
seven of your sheep last winter, and we
brought you the bloody fleeces, not being
able to save more, as we would fain have
done, for kind should be kindly."

" That is so," said the other two, with one
consent.

" You are good neighbours, and worthy
kinsmen," said Eormenred, who understood
Bosa, " and if you are glad, why so are we."

" Ay!" answered Bosa, with his head on
one side, like a simple-minded magpie.
" Ah ! but wherefore ?   Now will I come to
the point roundly and suddenly, for I am not
long-winded as you all know, but he that
would drag a load uphill, goes not up the
straightest track, but winds as he may for
easier draught, and if he be wise he has a
block to block the wheel, and let his horse
blow at times."

" That is so," chimed in the others as
before.

"You shall come to the point," said Eormenred, "at your leisure and discretion."

"I will ; and I know not how it is, but I speak with more comfort to you than to most, and the point is, this boy, my mother's sister's grandson. We are glad that he has come back with a good report, and is doing well of his wound. It is for his sake as much as on Sæbyrht's account that we are come ; our young folks are wild about him, and Leofgifu tells the mother that she will have him for husband or none."

"That is so," said the others, "but we were specially charged not to say so."

"Maidens begin to talk of husbands betimes in these days," cried Geatflæd severely, but Eomaer took her hand, saying—

"Why, mother, this is no new thing ; it is not as if I had never spoken to her." Then, turning to Bosa, he went on, not without blushes, "I will have Leofgifu if she will have me ; I told her so when she fought the fox which would worry her lamb. The snow was red with her blood before she strangled

the beast. It was in her thirteenth winter,
and now she counts fifteen."

" That is true," answered Bosa, "and the
marks are there to this day, spoiling the
beauty of her arms, the mother says."

" Spoil their beauty! What bracelet would
become her so well ? "

Then he whispered to his mother, who
made some show of reluctance, and ejaculated, "calf love!" but could not refuse her
son, and besides loved Leofgifu dearly. So,
after a little delay, she fetched something and
put it into his hand.

When the sons of Beorlaf rose to depart
from their kinsfolk, Eomaer delivered a ring
to Bosa, bidding him give it to Leofgifu as
a troth-pledge. Two golden dolphins boldly
embossed, supported a carnelian, on which
was carved the figure of a Naiad reclining
on a sea-lion, her limbs supported by the
finny coils of the monster, while she poured
drink which he lapped greedily.

" It is a pretty toy," said Bosa, "but here
is something fitter for a brave Gesith." He

took a bundle from the breast of his frock, and unfolding it, displayed a bright new seax, handsomely mounted, with haft of buck's-horn and sheath of pig's-skin.

" The king's smith made it of steel from these very forests. He says there is no over-sea metal tougher if it be well wrought. Let this be Leofgifu's troth-pledge, if father and mother agree."

There was no objection, except that both were so young, and early marriages were usual among the Saxons; so the betrothal was agreed to on condition that Eomaer remained five years among the king's Gesithas, unless there were good reasons for hastening the union; and therewith the sons of Beorlaf went home.

That night Leofgifu cut three long tresses of her bright hair and plaited them into a cord. On this she hung the ring, and knotted it about her neck, so that sleeping or waking she had her treasure on her heart.

CHAPTER XII.

RENATUS leaned against an alder stem which grew where a winding stream lost itself in a peat bog. The prospect was not alluring, but he looked at it, seeking matter to divert his mind from a more disagreeable subject of meditation.

Too much moisture was the evil in this place, while in another men and all living things were perishing of drought—one side of the world scorched, the other drowned. With proper distribution all might have enough, but excess and defect were alike ruinous. Is it true that there is a fixed, absolute, unchangeable amount of good to be divided among the sons of men, so that if one have more, another must have less? If the mighty river push out its delta into

the deep, the waves must wear away a cliff
elsewhere to restore the balance ; if the
torrid zone is a waste of sand from the intolerable heat, there must be an icy desert
in another direction, and beyond the frigid
barrier the happy, blameless Hyperboreans,
in contrast to our sinful, wretched world.
Dreams and fables ! — happiness is not a
matter of climate — and its distribution is
in His power who cannot err, nor be unjust.

Renatus kept his face studiously turned
away from a house built of logs, a few paces
distant from the spot where he stood, where,
in a shed, rested a litter with curtains closely
drawn, and the bearers crouched, sheltering
themselves from the rain.   His thoughts
struggled to enter the house, and see or
conjecture what was being done there ; but
he held them back, partly from repugnance
to the meeting he had himself brought about ;
and partly because he considered it whole-
some discipline to drive his ideas in his
own course, and not suffer them to wander
uncontrolled.

As with the gifts of fortune, so with the endowments of the intellect; beyond a certain point they confer no happiness. The lot of the wise man is not better than that of the fool. The ignorant sees not the consequence of what he does; he goes "as an ox to the slaughter, and as a fool to the correction of the stocks;" but the painful prevision of wisdom perceives the sluggish morass on one side of the path, the fatal precipice on the other, and what may be a lion in the obscurity beyond, but which proves to be only an inert stone or bush. Neither are wisdom and abundance good in themselves, nor are poverty and sickness evils ; rain is beneficial as sunshine, winter as summer, age as youth.

A faithful follower came to announce that the signal agreed upon had been made from the house. Renatus, absorbed in his reflections, looked at the messenger without seeing him, nevertheless the presence of another so far roused him that he continued his meditations in an audible voice, and the man listened dutifully.

"Where nature is bountiful man is usually indolent ; he who has most done for him, can do least for himself."

"Yes," replied the bearer, "those that mince their meat decay in their teeth. Dogs have good teeth, because they live on bones."

Within the house the interview had resulted in disappointment on both sides. When the time which had been so eagerly looked for came, and the mother held in her arms the child from whom she had been for years estranged, her emotion could find no words to express itself. Seclusion from the world had lamed her utterance ; there was little ground common to them both, and of that little only a fraction could be trodden with ease and safety. How could details of the past be told without showing Bronwen her father's baseness, her mother's guilt; it could not be. They sat in silence, weeping for sympathy, and Bronwen saw in the face by her side, years and sickness notwithstanding, such resemblance to the image

presented by her mirror, as assured her of
the truth of Renatus' statement. She essayed
a few questions, but the answers, broken by
tears and sighs, were hardly intelligible. At
length the mother, feeling that this was the
only opportunity that ever would be granted
to her, after inward prayer for succour in her
need, addressed her daughter—

" My sins prevail against me. I cannot
speak as I would. Fain would I help you,
fain offer counsel and warning ; for if the sins
of the parents are visited on the children, a
double penalty may well be yours. If you
could pass your days in some sacred seclusion,
in the company of a sisterhood of devoted
virgins, remote from the world, secure from
the wiles of Satan ; if some wise and holy
person would take charge of your innocence ;
but it cannot be, and I waste time in wishing.
My words must be few, for strength ebbs fast
away. Remember this maxim as my parting
gift, the only legacy your mother can bestow : ' Watch and pray.' Watch yourself,
pray for help and guidance. Self is your

worst enemy; think not of yourself, your
own wishes, your own pleasures ; seek rather
how you can do something for others—for the
poor, the sorrowful, the sick, the dying—as
you are doing now.   To-night, ere you sleep,
you will thank the good God that he has
enabled you to comfort one of his afflicted ;
try that each day a similar thanksgiving may
rise to Him from the altar of your heart.   To
see you was the one thing my soul craved,
and now that my desire is fulfilled, my speech
is hindered, my tongue tied.   Soon, perhaps
before this weeping day shall close, my spirit
will be far away, in the presence of a merciful,
pardoning Saviour, whose blood makes me—
yes, me—whiter than snow.   Turn to Him,
love Him, there is no love like His—none.
From heaven I shall watch over you ; doubt
it not.   But oh, my love, my darling, no
watching can avail, unless you watch yourself.
You have a father whom you love, and who
loves you—does he not ? "

Bronwen nodded assent.

" Think, when you are about to do anything,

'Should I like my father to know that I have done it ? ' But there is a Father in heaven who loves his children. Remember, that to him every action, every wish, every thought, lies bare and unconcealed ; that darkness is no covering from his eye. Cleanse your heart, beg Him to cleanse it by His Holy Spirit, that nothing may offend that pure and holy essence. Pray that rather the worst earthly ills may befall you, than that you should do what is evil in His sight. Now, dearest of all on earth, heart and breath fail me. One kiss, and leave me, for the anguish of parting is as the bitterness of death. God bless and keep you."

The same evening Howel Hên encountered with his grandson on the terrace roof of the bard's quarter. The young man was smart in his apparel, and had a sort of beauty—a red cheek, a dark eye, curling locks ; but withal a feebleness of manner and of expression, which provoked his grandfather's bile.

"Whither away?" the old man cried. "Whither are you bound with harp and scarlet feather, and—phew!—what a smell of unguents! What, in the devil's name, will you do with a ladder up here? Are you going to scale the firmament, and have a pluck at Ariadne's crown—will nothing less than Arianrod content you? Speak, man!" and he struck his stick impatiently on the pavement. "Speak! What owl's business are you about by the light of the crescent moon?"

"My purpose," the young man answered, "is to devote a starry hour to contemplation and the Muse. Silence and solitude——"

"And a ladder, are indispensable adjuncts to the inspiration of the poet," said the old man, mocking; then, with a sudden change of tone, and again striking the pavement with his stick—

"Why, you preposterous fool, you pernicious impostor, you deceitful, imbecile ostrich, will you bury your head in the sand when the horsemen are on your track—do you suppose that because I am your progenitor I can digest your lies. By the fathers, I know as well as you, perhaps better, the meaning of harp and feather, and that ineffable head of hair; and I am come to meet you, not for your hurt, but to comb your brains a little. In the first place, you are watched, followed. How could it be otherwise, when you cross from housetop to housetop, dark against a clear sky; and twangle that harp which you will never learn to play, to call careless passengers to your caterwaulings. Your fatuity would soon bring you to an untimely end if I did not look after you, for indeed I am better than a father to you except in sparing the rod."

Howel the younger had neither force nor spirit to stand up against the stream of language, and it was all the better for him that he could not. The old man paused for breath, and went on more mildly—

" So, seeing this sneaking villain prowling about, I desired to hear his voice and, running up against him by accident, ' Good man,' said

I, 'may I ask what, in the devil's name, you want here?' 'Avaunt!' he replied, 'avaunt, man of Belial!' I had a mind to break his sconce, but restrained myself, wishing to see the end, and pondering where I had heard his voice. Just then he raised his head quickly, and you crossed above with that ass's knowl which I should know among a thousand. Eat roses, so that peradventure you may be metamorphosed to a human aspect. You were the person my acquaintance was expecting, and he looked this way and that but saw not me. He crept to the door which leads to the garden of the women's court, and by the light of the blushing moon the flagitious monster took out a key, opened the wicket, and walked in. Inflamed by wrath and indignation at such an infraction of the law and the rights of the ladies, I lay in wait till the miscreant came out again, and smote him so heartily with my staff upon the crown that he dropped like a bullock. It was a cleric, not of those who follow our bishop, but one of the mad monk's gang; his head will ache when he thinks of the women's court for a year to come. So I took the key, and here it is. Go in by the gate to your mistress in a proper manner, and not over the walls like a thief. And now, hearken and heed, for this is a serious matter. In a few months, or weeks, or perhaps days, this city must fall ; the toils are closing round her, the hunters eager for blood and prey. These barbarians offer no quarter, and we should scorn to ask it. My master, whatever his faults, will die like a man, and I shall share his fate as my fathers have done with his fathers for a thousand years. The blood of Brut runs in his veins, albeit his great-grand-mother was a miller's daughter ; besides I am too old for new lords and new ways ;—as well die.

" For you it is different. You can do nothing in such a struggle as I see impend-ing. It needs no second sight to tell that our subjugation by the Romans was a gentle correction, a fatherly chastisement, compared to what will be suffered on all coasts accessible to the ships of these sea-wolves ; nothing but harrying, and burning, and slaughter, wherever and whenever there is anything to pillage. Armorica will be the safest refuge, the people are hardy and valiant, and for the most part of our own blood and speech. There you will be welcome, and I will give you letters to the colleges of the bards ; as will save something from the wreck if it be only the ancient name. If you can persuade the bastard daughter of the Count to accompany you, I will put you in the way of doing that also, and provide a bark and sufficient means. Are you man enough to attempt such an adventure ? Can you induce the lady to fly with you ? "

" I have little doubt that the lady will gladly accompany me to the world's end if I choose, but how do you reconcile such a plot with your boasted loyalty to the Count. Your conscience—— "

" My conscience and I can settle our affairs without your assistance. If I save his daughter from a frightful death and unite

her to the man of her heart, who shall blame
me? Is it my fault that the man of her
choice is a combination of ineptitude and
conceit? But mark you, my musical peacock,
other qualities will be needed to bring this
undertaking to a successful issue than those
you have hitherto displayed. A judicious
arrangement of cap and cloak, a flux of
croaking verses, and stale, misapplied flat-
teries will help you not at all; and you must
abandon your cherished scents, or the enemy
will hunt you like a fox. You will need
energy, promptness, courage, and judgment.
These I cannot give you, but what I can,· I
will do, that the name of Howel may not
perish from the earth. A small vessel, such
as you can easily manage, shall be in readiness, and the deaf and dumb boy will be in
charge of her. She will be stored with provisions, and you will find enough of the old
man's hoard to start you on the other side
of the sea, for they say that in a republic
nothing weighs against gold. The lady
must have all things in readiness, whatever

she may wish to bring with her ; for the time
of flight should be in the heat of the final
assault, before the Saxons are dispersed to
plunder.   This will probably be in the night,
and there must be no procrastination ; on the
morrow of that night, of all that you see
here, nought will remain but smoke and
ashes—the embers of our funereal pile."

Something in the old man's tone touched
Howel the younger, whose faults were of
the giddy head, not the bad heart, and he
said—

" Grandfather, I will stay with you and
bide the event.   It may not be so disastrous
as you anticipate ; but, come good, come ill,
I will not be such a dastard as to leave you.
The old house may end with me, it shall not
end in a coward."

" Well," said the old fellow, who was
pleased with this show of spirit, though he
could not refrain from snubbing, " I hope
not—in spite of your feathers and perfumes, I
hope not.   However, I won't be disobeyed
at my time of life, and you must do as I bid

you. Whatever I do and say is all for your good, as you will find." So saying, he marched off, little affected by his burden of years, hitting the pavement as if to show that his staff was rather an instrument of offence than of support, and his grandson, after attentively considering the key, went his way.

About the same time, Bronwen,. half sitting, half lying on a couch in her solitary chamber, thought over the events of the day. How much seemed changed since the morning, when she idly, angrily wished for something, anything to happen, which might break the monotony of daily life. Her wish had been fulfilled, and she uncertainly thought of the repose and security of the morning ; she did not regret it at present, but she might do so and with cause. Her susceptible nature had been moved by her mother's sufferings and tenderness, but her emotions were most often transitory. Renatus had visited her since her return, and had endeavoured to make more deep and permanent the impression already produced; but a scroll he had given her, lay half unrolled in the hand which rested in her lap. Its contents, and her mother's warnings, had given place before a movement of curiosity, an attempt to put together, in proper order, the scraps of information she had picked up, and to form a true conception of her actual position. She found the riddle more easy to read than might have been anticipated. Brought up among slaves, she had gathered the evil fruits of the tree of knowledge, and soon concluded from the allusions, more than once made, that her mother was not the Count's wife. What then? The only difference was that she knew her own condition, and could shape her conduct accordingly. The secret of her birth must have been known to the Count, and apparently to others, and had not injuriously affected her, why should it do so in the future. She could still look beautiful, and respond fervently to her father's pride and affection, and nothing more was required.

To her, thus musing and wondering, Fotis

entered with shoes and mantle, and remarked
that she had heard the harp, and had put the
lamp in the window. But Bronwen was
not going to the garden to-night, she had
promised, for her mother's sake, to do so no
more—it was not safe ; she had been ob
served, or more terrible still, Renatus, by his
magic art, had gained a knowledge of her
meetings with Howel, and this possibility
frightened her more than any other consideration. He might cause a hint to be dropped
in some quarter, and if detection should
ensue, her father, with his hot temper, might
renounce, imprison, kill her.

" I shall not go out to-night," she said to
Fotis. " I shall go to rest ; not immediately
—at the usual time."

Was it prudent to cast off a man really
bound to her, to anger him by refusing a
word of explanation or farewell ; besides he
was so stupid, he would go on harping till
morning, and draw on danger in that way.
Should she send Fotis to tell him that these
visits had better be discontinued till she

sent for him. He was capable of consoling himself with Fotis;—the thought was intolerable.

She stretched out her foot without saying a word, and Fotis put on the shoes; then, wrapped in the cloak, Bronwen crossed the terrace, and descended the steps which led to the garden. Though the rain had ceased, the night was overcast and dark, but the path was wide and well trodden, and she passed between dripping roses to the pergula, which was the trysting-place.

Renatus watched through the night by the couch of a sufferer, who lay with her hand pressed to her side, breathing hurriedly, and in the intervals of ease putting up petitions for the welfare of her beloved child.

CHAPTER XIII.

THE tower destined to protect the bridge from a boat attack was already fifteen feet high in some places, and growing rapidly. The landward side was curvilinear in plan, and protected by a trench filled with semi-fluid mud, more impassable than either earth or water. The rampart was formed of timber frames filled with logs laid with the narrow end inward, and having the interstices rammed with clay from the trench. The water face was rectangular, founded on piles driven deeply into the mud and braced firmly together. Between the piles faggots were thrust and on the faggots rubbish was thrown to sink them. This face was constructed entirely of wood, and at the height of twenty-five feet the platform was to be laid, on which the engines would work. On the piles of the bridge swinging cranes were so arranged as to be able to drop large stones on any boats which might succeed in passing the outer barriers.

Ælle had been up by night to examine the approaches to the bridge, but had gathered no information except an intimation that the Britons kept good watch. His boat, pulling muffled oars, came in contact with some floating matter which entangled the oars, and caused a noise which alarmed the guards. Lights were burned on both banks, and the catapults on the bridge took fair aim. Before the boat could be extricated from its awkward position several men were killed, and if one bolt had not stuck in a floor and so plugged the hole itself had made, the result might have been very unpleasant to the Saxon king.

He quickly determined to try if the other side of the bridge was as strongly protected, or if rafts, laden with combustibles, could be floated down on the ebb from that side. Having consulted with his sons, the most likely plan seemed to be that suggested by Cissa. He proposed that an expedition should be pushed out from the point where the fleet lay, and a place occupied where rafts could be made—a place easily victualled, easily defended, and not exposed to observation from the city wall. Accordingly, early on the morning of the calends of July, the seventeenth day from the beginning of this history, Brihthelm the sea-captain, accompanied by his sworn brother, Thorsten the tall, marched at the head of three hundred men to seek for a spot possessing all these advantages. They went by the seashore till they came to an estuary, one of the outlets of the river which encompassed Anderida. At low water it was a mere brook winding between broad, flat margins of mud; but when the tide was full, vessels of small draught could ascend it for a league or more. The expedition went up the right bank of this stream, bridging small affluents in their way

by felling soft-wooded trees which grew on
the brink, till they came to a channel too wide
to be crossed in that manner. Some of the
party swam across, and found themselves on
a long island, the farthest shore of which was
washed by the main river which ran down
to the city. The upper end of the island
was thickly wooded with ash and alder, and
seemed to fulfil all the conditions desired.
The part next the city was wet and used for
growing osiers, the whole extent of it being
at present uninhabited. Those who had
crossed, cut reeds and spread them in the
sun to dry, or collected dead wood and piled
it in heaps. Those who could not swim
made a light raft and twisted a strong bark
rope, by the help of which they crossed to
the other side with arms, axes, and provisions. Runners were sent back to the
camp with tidings of the successful lodg-
ment, and a request that boats and certain
necessary stores might be sent up by the
next flood.

There were no slack hands on the island;

some felled the longest and straightest trees,
others hewed off the tops and branches,
others cut withies in the osier-holt, and
twisted ropes to tie the raft-timbers together.
The logs were rolled to the waterside, but
were not made into rafts till everything else
was ready, lest the bands which held the
trees together should be loosened or broken
by lying unevenly on the mud at low water.
The trees to be used for each raft lay together with their notches cut, and staples
driven in, and only needed to be launched
and bound to each other. There were to
be fifteen rafts, each six fathoms long by
two fathoms wide, with a small mast forward,
and a space aft for six men to steer with
long sweeps; the central space was walled
on three sides with logs, but open aft, and
was filled with wood.

Ælle having heard that the expedition had
made a good beginning, proceeded to occupy
the attention of the citizens, and to give
them enough to do on his own side. He
marched out of his quarters with two thou-

sand men, and took a position between the camp of the men of Gwent and the fort which overlooked his own peninsula. Here he was attacked on both sides at once, but the broken ground was unfavourable for Farinmail's horsemen, and the Saxons found shelter from the arrows. There was skirmishing all day, but at sunset the Britons drew off, prepared however to fall upon .Elle, if, as they expected, he attempted to return to the sea. The Saxon king manifested no such intention, but appeared rather to contemplate a night attack on the fort. Farinmail, perceiving this, concentrated over three thousand men on the hills south of his camp, ready to seize the moment when the assault was fully developed, to take the assailants in the rear. Accordingly, a little before midnight, when from the uproar he concluded that the fighting was hot enough, he moved towards the scene of action.

The assault was sufficiently serious to require the full attention of the garrison, but the Saxons had reserved an adequate force to meet Farinmail as he mounted the ridge occupied by them.

As the hosts came within javelin-cast of each other, a man with a torch strode out from the Saxon line, and cried loudly—

"Is the Lord Farinmail among those who come against us?"

"He is here," answered Farinmail; "do you desire anything of him?"

"I do," answered the man with the torch, the light of which was too unsteady to show clearly the features of the speaker; "I desire single combat with you between the two hosts, that I may redeem the honour you took from me at the ford of the Adur."

"It is the Lord Æscwine who speaks, is it not?"

"It is, and it is from no envy or ill-will that I desire this of you."

"You speak and act courteously, now and always," answered Farinmail, "and in courtesy you shall be answered. Although I cannot admit that any honour was lost on the day of which you speak——"

"Mind what you do," said Comail, who did not care to stand by and see others fight, "or the Saxons may capture the fort in the meantime."

"It will not take longer," Farinmail replied with some vexation; "it will not take us longer to fight it out than if all were engaged."

"I don't know that," his cousin answered; "and then what becomes of your plan of taking them in the rear while they attacked the place?"

"Confound all plans," said Farinmail; "they always spoil the fun."

"Say you will fight him another day. It will be only a scuffle in the dark now. Sound the trumpets and set on; this is wasting time."

"Lord Æscwine," Farinmail said, "I was about to say, when I was interrupted, with what pleasure I should accept your challenge. I am told that it is too dark, that Ælle will take the fort while we fight, and that we can put it off till another season. It is only

things that are disagreeable which should be
put off till a future time ; therefore if you will
stand opposite to me we will fight in a crowd
now, and perhaps hereafter we may be so
fortunate as to meet in the manner you at
first proposed."

The trumpets sounded, and the two
champions exchanged a few blows, but the
hosts swayed this way and that, and forced
them asunder. The Saxons were less than
half the number of their enemies, as more than
a thousand of them were with Ælle against
the fort. They gave ground — but foot by
foot. The Britons overlapped them right
and left, but the triangular formation was
preserved, and all the heroism of Farinmail
failed to burst the array of locked shields.
Still the Britons pushed the wedge nearer
and nearer to the ditch of the fort, the din
was at the highest, and men fell fast on both
sides, when a lurid glare, and a dense smoke
which had for some time been increasing,
attracted Farinmail's notice ; it came from
the fort and blew straight in the faces of

the Britons, obscuring the faint moonlight. Thicker and more stifling grew the smoke, till Farinmail ordered the trumpets to sound again, and passed the word that each man should face to the right and follow his file-leader. This soon took them clear of the smoke, and rubbing their smarting eyes, they beheld a fierce fire dying down on the other side of the fort. Before they could comprehend the meaning of what they saw, cries arose within the fort, and a tumult — then dark figures came leaping from the wall, flying wildly towards the north.

While Ælle's attack upon the north-eastern corner of the fort drew all eyes to that quarter, a more unostentatious operation was being carried on at the opposite angle directly to windward. A double line of men lying flat on the ground passed baskets from hand to hand. A number of obscure figures at the foot of the hill put earth into these baskets, which went up full, were emptied into the ditch of the fort, and were then sent down the other line to be refilled. There

were also men in the ditch quietly levelling
the soil and treading it down. When a
sufficient quantity of earth had been accumulated, bundles of dried reeds were passed up
instead of the baskets, until a considerable
stack had been laid, which reached four feet
up the palisade of the vallum. The stratagem
had been already detected by the garrison,
who, distracted by the attack of Ælle on the
other side, only shot a few arrows and threw
a few darts, most of which lodged in the
bundles of reed which the Saxons held
before them. At length fire was applied, and,
fanned by the wind, soon crackled in a mass
of flame. The defenders of the fort could
not approach the fire, being to leeward of it,
and while the palisade was being consumed,
bundles of wet reeds were brought up from
the marshes below. When the palisade fell,
the wet bundles were thrown on the glowing
mass, which raised a prodigious smoke and
steam before it was extinguished. This was
the signal for Ælle, who came round in haste
and poured his whole force, twelve men

abreast, through the opening. He easily made himself master of the fort, slaying many of its defenders ; those who escaped joining Farinmail, who withdrew to his camp.

Contrary to the Saxon wont, Ælle occupied the fort, and on the highest ground within it pitched a lofty spar with a crow's nest on the top. Here the keenest sighted of his men by turns kept watch for a signal in a certain direction, smoke by day, fire by night.

To omit no means of preventing any exploration by the Britons towards the north, the fleet got afloat the morning after the taking of the fort. High water occurred about an hour after sunrise ; and the people saw from the walls sixteen ships advancing in line abreast. At first it was supposed that a simultaneous attack by land and sea was contemplated, but after a variety of manœuvres they came to anchor about a quarter of a mile from the walls, mooring themselves by the head and stern, ready for an advance when the tide turned about an hour and a half before noon.

Julius watched these proceedings with vague uneasiness; the cunning device which the Saxons had employed the night before was so unlike their ordinary, bull-headed way of doing things, that he apprehended some further display of wily contrivance. As soon as the loss of the fort and the manner of its capture were reported to him, the Praefect sent for Bael, but that worthy could nowhere be found. The ordinary scouts had no unusual intelligence to give.

The tide turned, but the Saxon fleet did not move. An old trading vessel was moored opposite the bridge, and seemed to be fitted as a fire-ship.

The Praefect went the round of the walls, examining every opening in the forest, and bidding the sentinels on the towers report immediately the slightest incident, whether they thought it important or not. Then he went to the new tower, which was rapidly approaching completion. Some felled the timber, some floated it to the bridge, some cut the tenons and mortises, some shaped treenails, while the most expert craftsmen hoisted up the beams and fitted them together in their places.

This tower was not at the end of the bridge farthest from the city, but rather less than half-way from the great gate to that point. It stood at the edge of the channel navigable at high water. From the tower to the earthwork which guarded its western extremity, the bridge crossed a sort of frog-land, where neither boat could swim nor beast walk; shallow pools and channels leading nowhere, overgrown with duckweed; islets of the consistency of hasty-pudding, clothed with all sorts of rushes and flags, where quick-eyed water-fowl lived pleasantly. That part of the bridge was secure from attack, even from approach of hostile bands, so at least Julius thought as he surveyed the country from the half-finished platform. While he speculated and wondered what would be the next move of the Saxon king, he saw an ecclesiastical person of humble degree coming from the city at a rapid pace. This man stopped where the new work bestrode the bridge, and asked for the Lord Praefect. Julius bid him come up to the platform. The man, scrambling over the piles of timber, mounted one of the ladders and delivered a double tablet, in which were written a few lines to the effect that the ordinary channel of communication with Pen y Coit was interrupted, and the messenger missing ; that a small party sent in that direction had not returned ; but that if the matter seemed important, any fresh tidings which came in should be forwarded to the Praefect.

" When did the missing runner leave here ? " Julius inquired.

" The day before yesterday," the clerk replied ; "and we know from another source that he reached Pen y Coit, and started thence on his way back yesterday morning, about four hours after sunrise."

" He may have met with an accident," Julius said, " or have fallen into the hands of robbers. Is there any special cause of suspicion ? "

" Not that I am aware of ; but our master
Renatus seems to suspect."

Julius smoothed the wax, scratched his
thanks, together with a request for any intelligence which came in, as no one could say
what was insignificant at the present moment.
Then he handed the tablets to the clerk, who
departed from him.

Long and earnestly the Praefect looked
northward, but could discover no doubtful
appearance, nor anything to guide his sus-
picions.   He looked towards Ælle's crow's
nest and observed a blue flag hanging from
it, then turning to descend from the platform
he saw in the opposite direction a thin blue
smoke curling above the tree tops about a
league away, just in the direction of the usual
route to Pen y Coit.   With a suspicion too
young to have definite shape, he ordered a
boat to be manned, bidding the men put their
weapons beside them, and sent for two
archers to accompany him.   While the boat
was being got ready, one of the workmen
standing by addressed him—

" If you go up to the stakes yonder, Lord Praefect, you might do well to find where all the chips came from that floated down thence with the ebb : there's heavy axe work going on somewhere yonder."

" Are you sure they were not made by our own men cutting trees for our own works ? Currents might carry chips up and down again."

" Not in such quantities as we saw this morning ; and besides," the man continued with the air of a critic, " no British axe made this chip. You see on this side the exact shape of the tool that cut it ; we fished out many, and most were cut with the same kind of axe."

" Go on to the platform one of you," said the Praefect, whose amorphous suspicion suddenly acquired head and tail. "Observe if there be any correspondence in colour or other particular between the smoke from the wood and the flags from the crow's nest, and let me know." So saying, the Praefect stepped into the boat ; but, before shoving off, he sent orders to different officials to collect boats, to bring the cranes to the other side of the bridge, and to alter the bearing of the engines on the walls. Also he sent messengers to Vortipore and to Farinmail, and was just starting, when a voice cried eagerly from the platform—

" A column of thick black smoke from the wood." .

" A black flag from the crow's nest," shouted another, as if answering.

" How is the wind ? " Julius asked.

" Down below here unsteady, but the clouds come from the north-east."

" When will it be high water to-morrow morning ? " he inquired again,

" About two hours after sunrise—rather less, perhaps."

Again Julius started, but once more paused to command all who were working on the tower to quit it, and to put together triangular wooden frames to protect the bridge from fire-ships.

The flowing tide carried the boat swiftly

up to the stakes, which barred the entrance to the main channel. There they reconnoitred both sides as closely as they could without going ashore, the water being high enough to allow them to row within ten or fifteen yards of the bank. They had just passed between the stakes, and were near a fallen tree, the head of which projected far into the water, when a large animal dived from it.

"What was that? It was too large for an otter," several cried at once.

At the same moment, a man with a javelin appeared on the tree; he was a Saxon, who, when he saw the boat, turned to retreat, but one of the archers shot him in the neck, and he fell into the water.

"Good shot!" said an approving voice from the other side of the boat. "That reptile has been hunting me these two hours. You may cut the eagle on priests," he said, wagging his head, "but you are too young to carve it on Bael."

Saying this the friend of Julius clambered into the boat, gave himself a shake, which threw off most of the water adhering to his greasy skin and raiment, and told the rowers to turn the boat's head and row lustily back, unless they desired to be "eagle-cut." As the boat approached the stakes, on its way back, Bael said—

"You need not wind about to pass them, they are all sawn through."

"Impossible!" exclaimed Julius. "We tried them as we came up."

"Try again," was the reply; "they are cut on this side; it was done this morning."

And bidding the men pull hard, Bael put his hand to the stroke oar, and sent the boat stem on to the stake, which cracked off and floated alongside, and they saw that only an inch of the oak was left uncut.

"What have you seen?" Julius asked. "What force have they?"

"Over four hundred men, perhaps five hundred. They have loaded rafts with billets of ash and pine, as much as they can get. These are laid crosswise, to let the flames get at them, round three sides of the raft, and the middle part is piled with dried reeds and brush higher than a man can reach. I saw barrels of pitch and of grease."

" How many rafts are now ready to start? "

" There were six of them perfectly ready, with seven men in each, and six long sweeps, and mast and sail. They will have the wind northerly by sunrise. These lie on a level flat of mud; there were six more close to the bank being filled with wood, and two or three more were being lashed together. They have a number of boats, which will carry from twelve to twenty men each. I saw two score and seven of them." As he said this, Bael stretched out his hands and feet twice, and then held up seven fingers, naming each finger in turn.

" We must attack them in boats," said Julius ; " there is no other way ; they would cut loose anything anchored to obstruct the channel."

" Yes," said Bael ; " and you must let me have half a dozen boats too."

The citizens watched on the walls all night. They knew that there would be nothing to see till the morning ebb, but there they stood in the damp, chilling mist. All night long, saws and axes and hammers sounded on the bridge, while the fires to light the workmen gleamed with a dim halo. A little before sunrise distant battle-cries were heard from the west, where Farinmail lay. As the warmth increased the vapours mounted upward, but they still lingered on the surface of the water, till the north-east breeze coming with stronger breath swept them away.

Then Vortipore and Julius, standing on the north-western tower, saw upon the water three rows of objects like floating haystacks, with a small sail to each, and two boats towing ahead—fifteen rafts and thirty boats. The British boats were close under the wall, ready to start when the foe came nearer. The flotilla moved more rapidly as the wind freshened, and the tide ran in a narrower channel. The signal was given –fifty British boats dashed off in a rather disorderly mass, and the Saxons, slipping the tow-ropes, advanced to encounter them. The two squadrons clashed together, and the Saxon vessels being smaller, several of them were stove, but the crews leaped on board other craft and fought quite at their ease.

Vortipore sent message after message, desiring that some of the boats should be sent after the rafts, but no one heeded. The jarring engines flung huge stones into the air, but those which fell among the stacks of brushwood seemed to do no harm. One made a happy hit, bursting the fastenings and loosening the timbers of a raft, so that the whole cargo fell into the water. The flames were beginning to leap among clouds of smoke, when six boats put off from the other shore—each fixed a grapnel firmly in the fore part of a raft, and began towing strongly towards the bank. The Saxons dropped their sweeps and tried to scramble over the burning pile to cut the tow-ropes, but it was in vain ; cunning old Bael landed all six rafts on a mud bank, where they burnt harmlessly, and made the survivors of the crews prisoners. As the other rafts came near the bridge, the men on board fixed the sweeps so as to give them the proper direction, and swam toward the western shore; but Bael was looking out, and slew most of them in the water. Then, having nothing more to do, he found a dry spot, and began torturing his prisoners, muttering as they groaned—

"Carve the eagle on Bael, will you? You are too young for that."

Of the eight remaining rafts, one was split in two by a projecting beam, and poured its burden on the hissing waters. The rest, impelled by wind and tide, crushed aside the hastily constructed defences, and lay against the bridge a mass of roaring flame. Some were sucked beneath the piles, where timbers and planking soon burned merrily.

The Saxons in the boats were severely handled by the superior numbers of the Britons, and gradually drew off when their work was done. They lost nearly two hundred men, and the Britons claimed the victory; but the fire-rafts had accomplished what they were sent to do. When the volumes of smoke rolled away, a double line of black, charred piles, showing more distinctly as the water fell lower, and some half-burned timbers caught by the boom below, were all that remained of a hundred and twenty feet of the long bridge.

CHAPTER XIV.

FARINMAIL had sustained an attack shortly
before the fire-rafts were set in motion—it was
a mere diversion, and was not persevered in.
After noon his scouts discovered that the
Saxons had withdrawn to their camp, aban-
doning the fort so recently captured. Farinmail at once reoccupied it, cleared out the
ditch, and renewed the palisade, marvelling
much at his good luck in recovering the place
so easily. The sentiment of astonishment
was vastly increased, when the following
morning revealed the fact that the peninsula
where the Saxons had lodged was utterly
deserted. Neither man nor beast, ship nor
boat, could be discovered, nor any trace of
the occupation but the trampled soil, the huts

and booths made of branches and reeds, and the ashes of the fires where supper had been cooked.

Farinmail laughed and sent word to Julius, who frowned, wondering what new stroke was in store for the city. Vortipore, who had shaken off his depression, and seemed disposed to bestir himself again, summoned a council when he heard the intelligence.

There seemed nothing better to be suggested, and the council met; but when the Count had opened the proceedings with a speech, in which he intimated pretty plainly that matters had been very grievously mismanaged during his enforced absence, and inquired what was to be done next, there was angry feeling displayed.

"At least, we have been doing all we could do," said old Gower, whose head was tied up with blood-stained bandages.

Etlym with the red sword, who carried his left arm in a sling, added—

"If every one had shut himself up for trifling hurts, our affairs would probably be in still worse condition. If you, Lord Count, do not approve of what has been done, suggest better plans."

" Certainly," the Count replied, " I do not approve of plans the result of which seems to be that we are hemmed within the four walls of the city. I find no fault in you, lords, who have done all that man can do, but I must regret that, for want of better guidance, your efforts have been futile. The head, not the hands, is to blame."

But the time was past to set the chiefs against Julius; the present peril was too imminent, and his skill was too well proved. He had assumed no state, interfered with no man's right; the old jealousies could not be revived. Cadogan rose, and said with some warmth—

" There can be no doubt that the ills which at present are come and coming upon us, result from the neglect of one chief—of him, namely, who, after the fight by the fords of Ouse (a battle won by the skill of another man), stooped after that marvellous, that

unhoped-for victory, to waste in ostentation ·
and perverse frivolity days which, properly
employed, would have yielded solid and permanent advantages. It is not worth while
now to recall how and by whom that great
opportunity was thrown away. We know
that time was given to the Saxons to recover,
and how the time was employed by them and
by us; and that our present evil estate is the
result of our apathy and their energy at that
crisis. We may most of us take upon ourselves part of the blame for that past neglect ;
but the heaviest load lies upon you, Lord
Count—you of all men are chiefly responsible
for the disasters which have ensued, for the
dangerous straits to which we are brought.
Instead of dangerous I should have said
desperate, were it not that he who alone
recommended vigorous action at the time to
which I refer, has shown such energy and
ability since, that faith in his capacity forbids
us to despair."

This speech was a heavy blow to Vortipore, who, as he looked round the table, saw

that every one present held similar opinions, both as regarded his own conduct and that of Julius. Madoc, formerly his assured ally, avoided his gaze and was silent. After a pause, he spoke—

" If after an illness which, though un-attended by outward wound, has been harder to endure than physical pain ; if after passing through conditions of mind which approached if they did not transcend the limits of sanity —conditions aggravated by the consciousness that my gallant friends were spending their blood and lives for Britain, while I lay useless and helpless ; if under these circumstances I have spoken unjustly, unbecomingly, at this our first reunion, I ask forgiveness. I will not excuse myself by pleading the fretfulness which comes of weakness, nor will I ask how many who now are quick to see my alleged mistakes, were as short-sighted as myself when clear vision was most needed. I will frankly say, lords, old friends, and fellow-soldiers, I spoke hastily, foolishly, ungratefully ;—forgive me, each and all."

Several hands were stretched to grasp those of the Count, which he held out right and left. After thanking each, he continued—

" To you, Lord Praefect, I must say something more. The Saxons, who but ten days ago were cowering behind the Adur, are before our walls, and yesterday burnt the bridge, in spite of all our efforts. They have now, we are told, vanished from our sight, to reappear, no doubt, under conditions most unsatisfactory to us. Without wishing to suggest that the measures adopted were not the best possible under the circumstances —without venturing to imply the slightest censure, or to allude in any way to what is past—I ask you to tell us candidly our present state as to men, material of war, provisions, and also whether there is any prospect of succour from without."

Julius rose promptly to reply, but there was a look of weariness in his eye.

" The city is victualled for three months, reckoning the actual population, and an additional garrison of two thousand fighting men, who should not be brought in till the last moment. As to men, we have three thousand two hundred outside the city, and Lord Farinmail has, I believe, over two thousand, of whom five hundred are horsemen."

"There are not five hundred now," Farinmail said.

"With the city guard we could put in the field six thousand well equipped and disciplined men. Ælle has with him now not more than four thousand five hundred men, including the sailors of his fleet. Besides these, the Count of Calleva has promised to come to our relief with three thousand warriors, and he may glean a thousand forest men by the way ; instructions have been sent to them to join him."

"And his Countship is recognised, I presume," said Vortipore.

"He uses the title allowed him by the Pendragon," Julius replied.

"If it were not so allowed," cried Farinmail, "to question his title now would imply

a condition of mind approaching if not trans-
cending the limits of sanity."

Vortipore looked sour, but said nothing,
and Julius went on—

"Our chief deficiency at present is in the
means of transporting large bodies of men
suddenly from one side of the water which
surrounds us to the other. We have between
fifty and sixty boats, which are capable
of containing about fifteen hundred men,
leaving barely space enough to work the
oars. Unfortunately, eighteen of the largest
of them draw four and a half feet of water,
and are useless, except where the water is
deep close to the bank, a rare contingency on
these flat, muddy shores. These have been
therefore applied to the restoration of the
bridge. Ælle is now probably somewhere
on the eastern side of the city, and if we
could suddenly throw six thousand men on
his straggling line of march, we might inflict
a loss—serious, perhaps irreparable. We
want the old bridge from the Praetorian gate,
but this is no time to rebuild it, nor do I

sec how it would be possible to contrive a temporary bridge of boats in the presence of such a foe as we have to deal with."

" Is there," Elphin asked, " any hope of succour from the Pendragon ?"

" There is a rumour in Venta," Farinmail said, "that he has been badly wounded in a great battle beyond the Severn."

" I have heard the report," said Julius, " and fear there must be some truth in it, or we should have had letters from him ere now."

The council broke up without having arrived at any definite conclusion, which was by no means an unusual event. The news of Ambrosius' wound awoke all the old ambition in the heart of Vortipore. If the hurt should prove fatal, who was nearer in the succession than himself? He felt that he had lost ground during this late period of seclusion, which it behoved him to recover without delay. The Count's power now rested solely on the confidence felt in him by the chiefs and people. His patrimonial estates, with the men who dwelled thereon, after being impoverished to the utmost, had passed to other lords ; his official dues had fallen to nothing. The city guard, amounting to nine hundred men, was in the hand of Julius, who could count besides a numerous train of armed clients devoted to him, while Vortipore's personal following—those who lived in the palace—were a short two hundred. The chiefs of the old British faction, on whom he mainly relied, had been alienated by his sloth and selfishness. Farinmail was disaffected. Perhaps he had been neglected. He must be reconciled, and something said about Bronwen.

He would invite everybody to a banquet. No, that would not do, it would be called ostentation and frivolity; besides, materials for the banquet might not be forthcoming. No, a dashing exploit ; what did the Praefect say about troops and boats, and cutting the Saxons in two ? It was worth thinking of, but it must be all his own. Julius should claim no credit for it.

Full of these thoughts, Vortipore went in quest of the bishop, whom he considered just now his trustiest adviser. He called two of the officers of the palace, who were also his distant kinsmen, and bid them take a few men and attend him. While a messenger went to inquire where the bishop could be found, Vortipore spoke to the officials, taking care that others heard what he said—

" It has been a dull time of late for you here, neither feasting nor fighting. I must give you all something to do now my health is somewhat restored. Would the men like more activity ? "

" I dare say they would," answered the elder officer, " but they do not complain on that score. What they grumble at is that the booty has not been distributed since the last battle."

" This is infamous," Vortipore exclaimed in great wrath at so straightforward a speech. " I will punish—I will punish most severely any one who defrauds my people ! Find out who is in fault, and you shall name the penalty to be inflicted on him."

" Better divide the spoil, that will give more satisfaction."

" That I shall do, of course," said Vortipore grandly; "and compensation shall be awarded for the delay, if I have to sell my daughter's jewels."

" We will win her new ones," said the younger man with enthusiasm ; but the elder, whose name was Tegid, put his hand to his moustache, and wiped away a smile.

" You shall not want the opportunity, brave cousin. Your noble words shall be remembered. Kind wishes may be as highly valued as generous deeds—aye, and as amply rewarded."

" Yes," the old fellow muttered, "and they are cheap besides."

" Then why are you so churlish as to grudge them ? " Vortipore asked with a laugh. " But I know you of old, cross-grained as oak, and as trusty. The spoil shall be shared, and a donative therewith. Hark ! 'boys," and the Count lowered his voice, "the Pendragon is wounded, perhaps

to death. If we lose him, which Heaven
forbid, it may be worth something to call
Vortipore cousin. I will not be dignified and
mysterious with my kinsmen. You all know
my pretensions, my rights; and you know
that what I have you share—that if I rise
you go up with me. I have been accused
of many faults, but not usually of meanness,
of keeping what I have to myself—eh, old
surly?"

"You were ever the golden hand," said
the young man.

"Lord Count," Tegid whispered, "if things
are taking such a turn, give me leave to
strengthen your household. We are little
above two hundred, counting the eunuchs; we
ought to be five hundred strong. There are
numbers of your old tenants who have little
cause to love their present lords; there are
hardy lads full of fight, who think a bird
in the bush worth two in the hand. I can
lay my hand on plenty such if I have your
permission."

"Do as you will," the Count replied; "only

one thing I stipulate—let no dazzling promises
of present pay be held out. The distribution
and the donative will exhaust my means for
awhile, and I will not be pledged to anything which it is not actually in my power to
perform. Truth—severe, unselfish truth—can
lend a lustre to the lowest station, and give
an added majesty to the very highest."

"Noble words, Lord Count," and Tegid
winked at his young associate a sceptical,
mocking wink, which filled the latter with
disgust.

The messenger brought word that the
bishop was at the Basilica, and added confi-
dentially that there was a controversy going
on.

They went to the Basilica, and entering by
a private door which led to the Count's seat
in the wing of the tribune, found that part of
the building filled with able-bodied young
clerics, each carrying a short, heavy cudgel
under his frock. Notwithstanding their
ecclesiastical garb and shaven crowns, they
did not look as if they would take a buffeting
patiently.

"A few score of these now," said Vortipore, "would not come amiss."

"You may count on the bishop's men,"
answered Tegid, "at need."

Down in the middle of the hall Renatus
stood on a bench gesticulating violently, but
not a word could be heard, the din seemed
somehow to obscure even the sight. The
orator threw out his arms, pointed to the
earth, raised his hands to heaven, shook his
fist at the bishop; his eyes flamed with
excitement, his thin nostrils were dilated,
and froth gathered at the corners of his
mouth.

The bishop rested his hands on the
marble rail of the tribune, and his big
shoulders heaved as he brought out his
words in a deep, clear voice, preferring
monosyllables when they could be used—

"If threats are hurled at me, fists shaken
at me, if I am defied, put to silence in my
own church, the blame shall not rest on me if
ill ensue. Words we will meet with words—
reason with reason—but if you appeal to the

arm of flesh, what can I do? There are those who came here hoping for crumbs of peace and instruction from my mouth—you curse and threaten them and me. There are limits to my influence, and to their forbearance."

A laughing truculence in the speaker's manner conveyed the impression that the limits were close at hand, and might in a moment be transgressed, and many in the crowd below were ready to meet their enemies half-way. But Renatus, trusting to his powers of speech, and deprecating fisticuffs as a theological argument, answered—

"We threaten no man. We tell you in all love and charity——"

"That if we do not keep Easter in your fashion; shave after your fashion, and in all things show ourselves your very humble servants——"

"And that for these crimes punishment is denounced, and our design is to warn you, that you may turn and repent, that you may escape——"

But some over-zealous friends of the old British Church suddenly lifted the other end of the bench on which the orator stood, and he disappeared in the surging crowd. The battle was begun ; the bishop's body-guard charged over the rails, and their pastor seeing that they had the upper hand, went to the Count's chair in the wing.

END OF VOL. II.